Praise for Tales of Truth and T
Child's Quest:

"Stormhaven is so appealing I'm considering searching for available properties on Rightmove. Mysterious pendants, Arthurian legend and a school in a castle. Utterly enchanting."

Kirsty Applebaum, author of *The Middler*, *Troofriend* and *The Life and Time of Lonny Quicke*

"I really enjoyed it and I can see that child readers of all kinds will love it too - from fantasy fans to myth-lovers to mystery-addicts to those who love school stories. Great stuff!"

Sophie Kirtley, author of *The Wild Way Home* and *The Way to Impossible Island*

*'*The Lost Child's Quest *is a heart-warming joy of a mystery novel. Its thrills are threaded with the myths and annals of ancient Britain, and its young protagonist, Tia, is admirable not only for her budding bravery, but also for being such a compassionate heroine. In fact, Haddell's entire novel thrums with kindness and empathy, and that's a wonderful thing."*

Darren Simpson, author of *Scavengers,* a Guardian Book of the Year 2019

"Superb! Full of mystery and history and erudition with the most incredible activities at the back. My daughter and I lay on the floor and listened to Adagio for Strings. *This book shines with love. I felt I was in the hands of a wonderful human being."*

Zillah Bethel, author of *The Shark Caller*

The Forgotten Crown

Tales of
Truth
and
Treasure
BOOK 2

JAMES HADDELL

Emira
Press

Published by
Emira Press
www.emirapress.co.uk

ISBN 978 1 91422 204 7
e-ISBN 978 1 91422 205 4

First edition 2021

*For all the families who have been brought together
by something more than birth and blood*

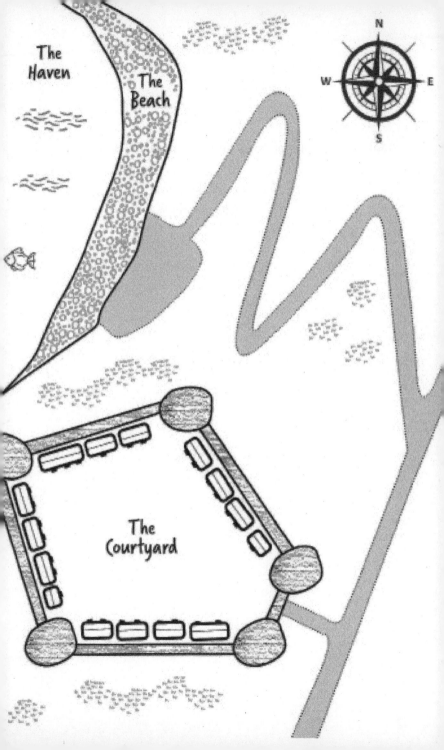

Chapter One

In the Cavern of the King

Tia Trevelyan stepped cautiously out of the gloom into a towering cavern lit by flaming torches set into the rocky walls. An enormous wooden table set for a single diner dominated the space and a fire blazed in a large alcove to her right. The crackling warmth of the flames and the smell of smoke could not entirely mask the damp coolness of the underground air, but it was comforting and reminded her of crowding around a bonfire on a cold November evening.

An old man sat before the fire in a throne-like wooden chair. Despite the brightness of the flames, his face was dark and shadowy. At first Tia was wary of him, but as she peered in she had the sense that some great sorrow was casting shadows across his face, and she began to feel saddened rather than threatened.

He was not nearly as old as he had first appeared either, but he slumped in his chair as if his shoulders were weighed down by more than just the heavy furs draped over them. His eyes looked weary, as though they had seen several lifetimes of sadness.

Tia edged forward until the man slowly turned his head to look at her. He gave her a tired smile, then spoke in a voice that was thick and hoarse. "I am glad you have come."

Surely this face hasn't seen enough days to acquire all the creases and scars etched across it, Tia thought to herself.

His smile faltered and he looked away, sighing as he continued. "I am done with war and destruction. All I ever wanted was peace for those I will leave behind. Had I known the cost of winning that peace, I am not sure I would have had the strength to pursue it." After a pause he gazed at her again and raised his thick, dark eyebrows. "Some call me king, but do you see a crown?"

Tia shook her head. Had she tried to speak, she knew she would have failed, for the sorrow in the room had stolen her voice.

"No, indeed." He stared back into the flames, looking disgusted with himself. "If I am king, then my rule has been a poor one. I am nothing but a lord of war and death. As many have died who followed me as stood against me. And now I think I shall not endure very much longer either."

He sighed and closed his eyes for a moment before looking up at Tia once more, with the faintest of sparks in his eye this time. "But with you, child, there is the promise of something new; of grace and peace and unity."

Tia felt far too small to be any of these things. She dearly wanted to ease the man's despair, but she knew she had no way of doing so. Yet still he gazed at her, as if he somehow expected all those beautiful things to burst out of her and chase away the shadows.

"But who *am* I? How can *I* possibly do all that?" she cried out at last, tears welling in her eyes.

And still he smiled.

"You, child, are—"

But his words were drowned out by a deep rumble and the cracking of rocks above their heads.

"Who *am* I?" she shouted again as debris began to rain down from the roof of the cave. The whole cavern began to disintegrate around her.

She could see the man's lips forming his silent reply before he faded into a cloud of dust. She clutched at the scene with her thoughts as well as her hands, trying to visualise the lines on his face, but the very memory was slipping through her fingers like tendrils of fog.

Then something struck her on the shoulder and she awoke.

Chapter Two

Tia's Journal

Meghan was trying her best not to wake Tia, but quietness wasn't her greatest strength. She had done quite well to start with, tiptoeing around her sister, who was asleep on the floor, but she lost her balance as she was pulling on her socks and had stepped on Tia's shoulder.

"Sorry!" Meghan hissed, spinning around, losing her balance again and very nearly stepping on Tia's nose with her other foot.

Tia groaned in response, trying to give the impression that her sister hadn't completely woken her up before pretending to go back to sleep. Meghan found her glasses, tied her thick hair back with a green bandana and left the room with relative stealth.

Their cousin Alfie's bedroom, where they had been sleeping for a few days since arriving in London, was quite a bit smaller than the girls' bedroom at home. Tia's aunt and uncle lived in a two-bedroom apartment overlooking a small marina on the south side of the River Thames. Alfie, who was a few years older than Meghan and Tia, was away on a school rugby tour travelling around the south coast, so the girls were staying in his room while Mr and Mrs Trevelyan slept on the sofa bed in the lounge. Having taken Alfie's bed, with Tia on the floor, Meghan had been finding it very hard not to disturb her sister in the mornings.

The family had travelled to London as soon as the Christmas holidays began. The main reason for the trip was to view the Kirkburn Sword at the British Museum, which Tia and her best friend Pasco Penrose had discovered a few weeks earlier, but they had stayed with Mrs Trevelyan's sister for three nights and seen some of the other sights London had to offer. They were to spend their final day at the Tower of London, where Uncle Ernie worked, before heading back to Stormhaven for Christmas.

After a minute or two Tia got up and dressed, then spent a few moments gazing out of the window at the boats moored in the marina. It wasn't quite the same as the view she had from her bedroom window at home, but there was still something very calming about looking out over a body of water.

Tia had lived in a children's home until she was almost ten, and despite the sense of belonging she now felt as part of the Trevelyan family, she usually still woke up with a hollow sensation in her stomach. It was as if feeling anxious had become a habit, developed by the most primal parts of her brain in those first few years when she hadn't known the love of a family. It was a habit that was proving hard to break.

Looking for something familiar to hold as a way of grounding herself, Tia traced her finger over the X symbol carved into the simple silver pendant she always wore and picked up the journal she used to write down all the snippets of information she gathered about her 'quest.' This had begun as a quest of self-discovery, following the meagre clues she had with regard to her birth history, but somehow it had led to her discovering the legendary Thirteen Treasures of Britain. Now Tia had been given another quest.

She flicked through her journal to the pages where she had written down the message delivered to her by the guardian of the Thirteen Treasures, Sanddef; words that had become so familiar to her that she could have recited them in her sleep:

The guardian's message from Merlin/Myrddin:
With your coming, the time is now at hand
for the Hallows of Arthur to be gathered
for unity not division; for love not war;

for creation not destruction; for grace not law.
This is your task: to gather the Hallows of Arthur.

Tia stared at the name 'Arthur' for a moment and could almost picture him as a noble but battle-weary chieftain. In her mind he was gazing at her as if he knew who she was.

She sighed and read the next three words:

Stone. Oak. Circle.

This was not the whole second part of the message Sanddef had intended to give her. They had been interrupted, and he had only had time to speak these three words before throwing Tia and Pasco to safety as the underground cavern they had been standing in collapsed around them.

If only Sanddef had been able to relate the whole message before Mr Silverman arrived and tried to stop them, Tia thought to herself for the hundredth time. As ever, this thought was soon followed by, *I wonder if Pasco has any new ideas about what all this means.*

Tia was longing to get back to Stormhaven to speak to her friend, but not just in the hope that he had deciphered these riddles; she simply missed him. She had loved spending time in London. As well as visiting the British Museum, they had seen Buckingham Palace and the dinosaurs at the Natural History Museum, and it had been wonderful getting to know her aunt and uncle a little. But Tia belonged at Stormhaven now, and she smiled every time she thought of the castle, the school and the little village, and especially Pasco and her Grandpa Locryn.

Nana Ollie was also in Stormhaven at the moment. The Trevelyans' house had been her base while she travelled around the country, catching up with friends and finding homes for some of the treasures she had unearthed during her diving expeditions in the Caribbean. She would be heading back there after Christmas and Tia was eager to spend as much time with her as she could before she left.

Tia shut the book and slipped it back inside her bag. They would be leaving for the Tower of London straight after breakfast, and after that it would be a quick turnaround before they headed home, so she decided to pack up her things right away. After rolling up the camping mattress she had been sleeping on, Tia went off to find the rest of her family.

Chapter Three

The Tower of London

Tia's parents and sister Meghan were eating toast and drinking orange juice on high stools around the breakfast bar with Uncle Ernie and Aunt Kensa.

"Ah, Tia," said Aunt Kensa, rising to her feet. "I was hoping I'd get to say goodbye before I left for the office."

Aunt Kensa was like a slightly less laid-back, but no less warm and smiley, version of Mrs Trevelyan, and Tia had liked her at once.

"It's been wonderful getting to know you," she continued, putting on her long black overcoat and wrapping a thick turquoise scarf around her neck. She walked over to Tia, kissed her on the forehead and whispered, "Welcome to the family." Then she said goodbye to the others and left for work.

It had taken Tia longer to warm to Uncle Ernie, who had a mop of scruffy grey hair and wore spindly glasses that looked as though they were about to slide off his crooked nose. He had the air of someone whose mind was always on something else. Tia had the sense that he would have preferred to *be* somewhere else most of the time, but she soon came to understand that he was simply a little absent-minded.

He was munching a slice of toast and reading the newspaper while Meghan tried to have a conversation with him about what they would see at the Tower of London that morning.

"And the Crown Jewels are kept in their own special room, is that right?" Meghan asked excitedly.

"That's right," Uncle Ernie replied without looking up from his newspaper. "They're kept in the Jewel House at the Waterloo Barracks."

"And that's where you work?"

"That's right." He turned a page but still did not look up. "I'm in one of the back rooms working with the old crown records."

"I thought you were the one guarding the jewels," said Tia as she took a seat at the breakfast bar and helped herself to a slice of toast.

"Nothing quite that exciting, I'm afraid." Uncle Ernie

looked up this time and raised his hairy grey eyebrows in Tia's direction. "I do guard almost a thousand years of national history in those archives, though!"

Tia tried to look impressed but wasn't entirely sure she had managed it.

Once everyone had eaten breakfast, they wrapped themselves up warmly in hats and scarves and headed out into the crisp wintry morning. It was always a bit of an effort to restrain Tia's thick, dark red curls under a hat, and she could feel her locks trying to push it off in a bid for freedom as soon as they stepped outside.

There was a pier at the end of the road, where they hopped aboard a boat that ferried commuters up and down the river. It was only about a ten-minute ride to the Tower and they were able to enter the ancient castle with Uncle Ernie before it opened to the public.

The plan was for the Trevelyans to spend the morning exploring the Tower before Uncle Ernie gave them a tour of some of the areas that were off-limits to tourists. Then he would take them for lunch at his favourite little café just outside the Tower gates before they began their journey back to Stormhaven.

"Okay, then?" said Uncle Ernie as they reached the steps of the building where he worked. "I'll meet you back here at midday." He glanced up and groaned. "Oh, not him again!"

Tia followed her uncle's gaze to see a hunched old man with bushy grey eyebrows and an even bushier grey moustache standing there. He wore a black cap, a long brown coat and a pair of thick, round glasses that magnified his eyes. He was clutching a battered brown leather briefcase in one hand and a walking stick in the other as he slowly but determinedly made his way across the courtyard toward them, grinning broadly.

"A French chap who turned up last week, pestering me about viewing some old jewel account records from the reign of Edward I," Uncle Ernie explained quietly, the annoyance clear in his voice. "He was perfectly charming at first, and I even took him into some of the rooms that aren't usually open to the public, but it soon became clear that he actually wanted to view and handle specific documents. I explained that I couldn't allow that of course but that hasn't stopped him coming back and trying again several times. He's harmless enough and perfectly polite, just very persistent." Uncle Ernie sighed and went to greet the Frenchman. "Monsieur Moreau," he called, "you'll have to invest in a season ticket if you keep coming back so often!"

"Come on," said Mr Trevelyan, placing an arm around each of his daughters. "Let's have a look around."

Mr and Mrs Trevelyan wanted to take their time going round each section of the Tower and grounds, so Meghan and Tia were allowed to go off to explore at their own pace. After visiting the White Tower and several of the other buildings in the courtyard, the girls decided to head over to the Jewel House to see the Crown Jewels.

Tia and Meghan's relationship had turned a corner in the last couple of days. Meghan had felt guilty for the part she had inadvertently played in landing them all in peril during their hunt for the Thirteen Treasures of Britain, so Tia had confided in her sister certain details of the adventure that only she and Pasco knew. She had shared the message Sanddef had given her about the Hallows of Arthur and the fact that she had actually retrieved one of the treasures: the Mantle of Arthur.

"Wow," Meghan had gasped in response to these revelations. She had assured Tia that she wouldn't breathe a word to anyone, and Tia had promised to show her the cloak – which was safely tucked away under her bed at home – once they returned to Stormhaven.

"The Crown Jewels were first kept at Westminster Abbey and Edward I moved them here in 1303," Meghan said, skim-reading the guidebook as they made their way across the courtyard in the direction of the Jewel House. "But those Crown Jewels were either destroyed or lost after the Civil War, apart from three swords – oh, and a spoon – so they made new ones after that. What are you looking at?"

Tia had stopped in her tracks and was staring at a figure that had slipped behind the corner of the building they were approaching.

"I think I just saw that Frenchman sneaking around the corner," said Tia with a puzzled expression on her face.

"Shall we see what he's up to?" Meghan asked, trying to hide her delight at the prospect of doing some detective work but completely failing.

The two of them hurried over to the corner Monsieur Moreau had just disappeared behind. Peering around it, they saw the old man press himself up against the wall next to the fire exit, check his watch, then crouch down. It occurred to Tia that he was moving a lot more nimbly than he had when he approached Uncle Ernie earlier that morning.

But Tia's thoughts were suddenly interrupted as an alarm bell rang out from inside the building, shattering the still morning air.

Chapter Four

A Mysterious Discovery

Tia looked behind her, where scores of tourists were streaming out through a side door and down the steps where the Trevelyans had arranged to meet Uncle Ernie at midday. Looking back in the direction of Monsieur Moreau, several people who looked like staff rather than tourists began filing out of the door the Frenchman was crouching behind.

Once the last of them had exited the building, Monsieur Moreau coolly hooked his walking stick around the edge of the door as it was about to shut. He waited a few seconds to make sure none of the Tower staff looked back in his direction, then silently rose to his feet and snuck through the doorway. Tia and Meghan instinctively sprinted towards the door to prevent it from shutting fully behind the Frenchman.

Catching hold of it just in time, Tia looked at her sister and two options ran through her head: shout to alert someone to the intruder's presence or follow him themselves. It was clear that only one option had occurred to her adventurous sister. Grinning broadly, Meghan raised a finger to her lips and slowly opened the door.

The sisters peered in just as Monsieur Moreau's heels disappeared around a corner. They slipped inside and rushed after him as quickly as they could, trying not to make any loud noises. They need not have worried about making a sound, as the alarm, which was still echoing through the corridors, was enough to drown out much more than the scuffling of their shoes.

Again, it struck Tia that the Frenchman was moving much more quickly than she had expected after seeing the old man hobbling across the courtyard towards Uncle Ernie earlier that morning. They followed him round a couple more turns until he stopped outside a solid-looking door. He laid a gloved hand on the handle and turned it. Monsieur Moreau let out a happy sigh, clearly relieved to have found it unlocked.

He opened the door a crack and peered inside, as if to check that there was no one on the other side, then opened it fully and walked through.

Meghan leapt forward and deftly caught the door

handle so that it pulled to without shutting fully. Tia snuck up beside her, and they opened the door a crack, just as Monsieur Moreau had.

The room appeared to be some sort of old library at first, but Tia noticed that the rows of tall wooden cases housed hundreds of wide drawers rather than books. The old man was slowly making his way down one aisle, examining the labels on the drawers as he went. Once he was out of sight, Tia and Meghan opened the door just wide enough to creep inside.

The alarm was still sounding, but unlike the corridors this room was carpeted, which helped to muffle the relentless ringing a little. The girls tiptoed over to the end of the row Monsieur Moreau had walked down. They peeped around the corner to see him gazing triumphantly at the drawer in front of him.

He pulled it open and chuckled in a very self-satisfied way. Without taking his eyes off its contents, he drew a pen-sized torch from his jacket pocket. He adjusted his glasses and shone the light on whatever it was in the drawer that seemed to have excited him so much.

Tia frowned in curiosity at the colour of the light shining from the torch. Rather than the white or yellow she had expected, a strong, purplish glow was lighting up the drawer and illuminating the old man's delighted face. Perhaps it was his grin, or maybe it was the easy manner in which she had seen him move along the deserted corridors, but he seemed decades younger than when he had shuffled across the courtyard, even with the strange light outlining every line and blemish on his face.

Just then, the alarm stopped. Startled, Monsieur Moreau looked up and glanced back towards the doorway. In a flash, Tia and Meghan jumped back behind a row of cases.

"Did he see us?" Meghan asked in a breathless whisper.

Tia didn't know, but instinct told her they should move elsewhere just in case. She nudged her sister, and as quickly and silently as they could, the two girls scampered behind the neighbouring row of drawers so they were two aisles away from Monsieur Moreau and the mysterious drawer.

Tia heard movement, as though the old man had shuffled to the end of his row to check if anyone was there. *He must have seen us*, she thought, willing her lungs to breathe more quietly. She slowly peered around the end of the row of cases, venturing a glance with just one eye.

Her blood ran cold as she saw one of Monsieur Moreau's eyes doing exactly the same thing, peering directly at her around the corner of his aisle. She gasped and heard him do likewise. She expected him to dash towards them, and was about to grab Meghan's arm and run in the opposite direction, but instead he sprinted towards the door.

Meghan reacted instantly. "Hey!" she shouted, bolting after the fleeing man.

But he was closer to the door than the girls. He

got there ahead of Meghan and slammed the door in her face. She frantically tried turning the handle and throwing herself against the door, but Monsieur Moreau was evidently holding it shut or had barricaded it in some way.

Meghan started banging on the door and shouting while Tia looked down the aisle where the Frenchman had been. The drawer was still open, and lying on the floor in front of it was the strange, purple-coloured penlight, still shining. Tia hesitated, but her curiosity was too great. She picked up the light, clicking it off as she moved to peer into the drawer.

Inside lay the most ancient-looking piece of paper she had ever seen. The faded writing was hard to make out, but one word caught her eye: 'Arthur'.

Ever since she had been given the message by Sanddef concerning The Hallows of Arthur in the Chamber of the Thirteen Treasures, the name Arthur had never been far from her thoughts. Tia felt the hairs on her neck stand up, as if they too were eager to see what this parchment had to say. She glanced at the other words, many so faint and scrawling that reading it was a little like listening to someone speaking down a crackling phone line.

Coron Arthur... presented to King Edward at Cymer upon defeat of the Welsh 1283... Llywelyn's Coronet recoated... Coron Arthur presented at Westminster Abbey... Coronet retained with the royal regalia.

Tia hadn't the slightest idea what a coronet or a coron was. In fact, she had very little idea what any of it meant. Then she remembered the penlight she had picked up. She switched it on and shone it onto the ancient parchment. The sight that met her eyes almost caused her to drop it in shock.

Chapter Five

The Coron Arthur

Meghan's continuous banging on the door eventually attracted the attention of the Tower staff, who began filing back into the building once the fire brigade had confirmed that there was no danger. Apparently, it had been a false alarm, set off at the opposite end of the building. By the time the girls had explained about the intruder, no trace of Monsieur Moreau was to be found.

While Meghan gave a very vivid account of the incident to security staff, Tia led Uncle Ernie and Mr and Mrs Trevelyan over to the parchment that Monsieur Moreau had been so interested in. When she showed them what the Frenchman's light revealed, Uncle Ernie turned white and was unable to speak for several minutes.

"I'll get you a drink, Ernie," Mr Trevelyan said.

While her father went to fetch a glass of water, Tia directed a couple of the questions that had been fizzing through her brain at her mother.

"Do you know what a coron is?" she asked. "Or a coronet?"

"They're basically the same thing – a crown," Mrs Trevelyan answered, glancing at Tia before looking back at Uncle Ernie, as if worried he might faint at any moment.

A crown of Arthur, Tia thought for a moment before asking another question. "And why does this other writing only appear under the purple light?" She shone the penlight on the parchment again. Many more markings appeared on the page under the strange glow. Most were nondescript blotches and scratches, but one purplish sentence shone out from what had previously been blank paper:

Coron Arthur interred at Glastonbury Abbey by King Edward himself, 1303.

"Sometimes when you shine ultraviolet or infrared light on documents it shows things that are not visible to the naked eye," Mrs Trevelyan said. "It's amazing what can show up: things written in invisible ink or things that have been erased. Paper hasn't always been as widely available as it is now, and pieces were sometimes wiped blank to be used again. It's best not to shine too much light onto such old documents, though, Tia."

Tia switched off the penlight, put it in her pocket and said, "This bit looks like it was part of the rest of the writing, though. It's as if someone's just rubbed out the last line; like they wanted to keep it a secret."

"Yes," Mrs Trevelyan said thoughtfully. "It certainly does look that way."

"The record was always a little ambiguous." Uncle Ernie had found his voice again but spoke in a croaky sort of whisper. "I always thought Llywelyn's Coronet and the Coron Arthur were different names for the same crown – a crown that was believed to have belonged to King Arthur and handed down the line of Welsh princes until Edward I conquered Wales and took possession of it. However, this parchment seems to confirm that they were separate items, and that the Coron Arthur was taken to Glastonbury rather than being kept with the Crown Jewels." He puffed out his cheeks and shook his head.

Mrs Trevelyan also let out a sigh, apparently reassured by the return of his speech, which indicated that Uncle Ernie was no longer about to pass out.

"Remarkable!" Uncle Ernie exclaimed.

After a thoughtful pause, Tia said, "But *why* would someone want to keep what really happened to the Coron Arthur a secret?"

"I suppose," Uncle Ernie mumbled almost absent-mindedly, still staring at the parchment, "to protect it."

By the time her father returned with a drink for her uncle, Tia was already wondering whether the crown might have something to do with the quest she had been given to gather the Hallows of Arthur. All she really knew for sure about her task was that she needed to look for items connected with the real Arthur, and this was the most promising lead she had stumbled across so far. Perhaps there was some way of tracking down the Coron Arthur.

"What does it mean when it says, '*interred* at Glastonbury Abbey'?" she asked.

"It's a bit confusing trying to piece all this information together," Mrs Trevelyan replied. "When we get home, I'll get out a few books, check some dates and explain things a bit better."

Tia would have to wait for answers. *No change there, then*, she thought to herself.

Once Tia and Meghan had given their reports to the Tower security guards, the Trevelyans said goodbye to Uncle Ernie, who had to stay back and work through his lunch break. After grabbing some food, the Trevelyans caught the boat back to the apartment to collect their bags, then set off home to Stormhaven in their little purple car.

For the rest of the day, Meghan chatted away enthusiastically. She talked about how they were going to spend the Christmas holidays, what they still needed to do with Nana Ollie before she left and their upcoming trip to Aberystwyth, where they hoped to learn more about the late Professor Hemyke and his connection to Tia. Mostly, though, she talked of the mystery surrounding Monsieur Moreau and the Coron Arthur.

"Do you think he's going to try to steal the Coron Arthur?" Meghan said, suddenly sitting bolt upright as they waited in traffic on the A303. "Dad, we need to call Glastonbury Abbey and warn them!"

"I don't think there's any need for that," her mother replied calmly. "Glastonbury Abbey was demolished in the sixteenth century by Henry VIII, and all that remains now are ruins. There's no way of telling what became of the Coron Arthur."

Meghan, who had clearly been hoping for a bit more drama, instantly deflated, and Tia's heart sank a little.

Chapter Six

The Black Marble Tomb

Tia loved the village of Stormhaven. Just driving through the castle gatehouse made her feel at home, but it was only ever on passing through their own front door that she was able to feel completely at ease.

Decked out in Christmas decorations, and with Nana Ollie waiting to greet them, the house was especially warm and exciting on this occasion. Excitement and anxiety, however, are often two sides of the same coin. The buzzing anticipation of Christmas also made Tia feel tense and slightly on edge. This strange mix of emotions made it impossible for her to know precisely how she felt.

As soon as Meghan was through the door, she began rummaging through the bags they had brought with them from London, looking for the wrapped Christmas presents they had been given by Aunt Kensa and Uncle Ernie. She had a permanent grin etched across her face as she carefully placed each one under the Christmas tree.

Tia looked at her sister with envy at her ability to feel only the excitement of the season. *Maybe the anxiety just affects her differently,* Tia thought as she observed Meghan's inability to settle in one position for more than ten seconds over the next couple of days, though in truth she was never normally stationary for more than five minutes at a time anyway.

The mood was entirely different on Christmas morning. The two girls sat with their parents and grandmother in the living room, unwrapping presents while they themselves were wrapped up in dressing gowns. As she ripped the paper from her gifts, Tia felt as if she were tearing away the thin layers of tension that had been enveloping her.

She found herself in something of a relief-induced daydream as she sat through the short Christmas service Grandpa Locryn presided over in the chapel later that morning. Grandpa Locryn then joined them for Christmas lunch, and for the rest of the day they played noisy board games and ate Christmas treats.

Tia slept in on Boxing Day morning. When she finally entered the kitchen, she found her mother sitting at the table surrounded by several large books displaying pictures of medieval kings and various diagrams of royal family trees.

"Morning, Tia," Mrs Trevelyan chimed as she set a cup of coffee down between the books. "Your dad, nana and sister have gone out for a morning stroll. I've been looking up a few things about the Arthurian legends of Glastonbury Abbey. Fancy a Boxing Day history lesson?"

Tia wasn't entirely sure she did, though she certainly wanted to know more about the Coron Arthur and its connection to Glastonbury Abbey. Her mother also seemed very excited at the prospect of giving her a history lesson, and Tia didn't have the heart to disappoint her.

"Okay," she replied, rubbing the sleep out of her eyes, and pouring herself a bowl of cereal.

"Well," said Mrs Trevelyan, "we should probably start with 1066."

"The Battle of Hastings?" Tia exclaimed, glad to be starting with something she knew, but already confused as to how that fitted with the story of the Coron Arthur.

"Indeed. The Normans invaded from France in 1066 and very quickly conquered England, but they spent the next few hundred years trying to extend their rule westwards and northwards towards the more Celtic parts of the country."

"Like the battles Arthur had with the Saxons you were telling me about a couple of months ago?" Tia asked.

"There certainly are a lot of similarities," said Mrs Trevelyan, grinning broadly, "though this was a conquest from the start, whereas the Saxons were more like migrants to begin with. The battles with British Celts didn't come until later. Stories of Arthur had been passed down by the British people for centuries. There was a belief among the British people at the time of the Norman conquest that Arthur wasn't dead, but was instead sleeping in a mythical place called Avalon and would one day return to save Britain. This was a source of hope for the Britons, especially those who were not fully under Norman rule: people in Wales, South West England and the North."

"But how does Glastonbury Abbey fit in?" Tia asked with a mouthful of cornflakes.

"Well, in 1191 the monks at Glastonbury Abbey – which was very much in *Norman* England – announced that they had discovered the remains of Arthur and his queen, Guinevere. Two coffins were supposedly dug up along with a lead cross, which bore an inscription in Latin saying who they were, and that Glastonbury was the true Avalon." Mrs Trevelyan pointed to one of the open books, which featured an illustration of the lead cross.

Tia wasn't quite sure what to make of this. The Arthurian legends felt as closely linked to her now as the legend of the Thirteen Treasures of Britain had a couple of months earlier. On the one hand, she desperately wanted to gather all the evidence she could that Arthur was a real historical figure, but she also wanted to believe that there was some truth behind the incredible Arthurian myths. Somehow, an Arthur who had died, been buried and then dug up by a bunch of monks a few centuries later didn't seem quite right.

"Most historians think the 'discovery' of King Arthur's Tomb was a deliberate hoax," Mrs Trevelyan continued. "Glastonbury Abbey was running out of money before the grave was discovered and began to do very well from all the publicity afterwards. The Norman rulers also made the most of this discovery. Arthur having a burial site pretty much proved that he wasn't going to return to save the people of Britain, and it gave them a chance to identify themselves with the legendary King Arthur. This was the start of the Normans trying to make Arthur a symbol of their new Norman-ruled England rather than a symbol of the old independent, Celtic Britain.

"Edward I was just one of several English kings who made sure to link themselves to the popular legends of King Arthur. Almost a hundred years and a few Norman kings after the discovery of the grave, he personally moved Arthur and Guinevere's bones to a special new tomb made of black marble that he had ordered be built in the most prominent position in Glastonbury Abbey. Given what you learned at the Tower of London, we now know that he later placed the Coron Arthur in the tomb after he defeated the Welsh."

"But then the abbey was destroyed?" Tia screwed up her face in concentration as she tried to piece all the information together.

"Yes." Mrs Trevelyan pushed a book with a photograph of ruined stone arches and pillars towards her. "Centuries later, Henry VIII took ownership of England's abbeys and had them stripped of their wealth. There's no record of what happened to the bones in the black marble tomb or to the Coron Arthur."

Tia sighed. It all just about made sense, but only just. And it was enough to convince her that the Coron Arthur might really have belonged to *her* Celtic Arthur…

But where on earth is it now?

Chapter Seven

Go on Adventures!

The day after Boxing day, the Trevelyan family offered to help Nana Ollie carry her bags into the castle courtyard, where a taxi would be waiting to take her to the airport. As they walked, Meghan bounced with excitement as she asked about her grandmother's next planned diving expeditions and what she hoped to discover. Once the taxi was in sight, however, they all felt the weight of this last moment spent with someone they loved dearly before a long separation.

"I'll see you again soon, I promise," Nana Ollie said, holding her two granddaughters close. "I have something for you both; a kind of to-do list for life." She pulled two identical cards from her pocket and handed one to Meghan and the other to Tia.

"If everything you ever do ticks at least one of these boxes, you'll be happy." She spoke evenly, but tiny tears twinkled on her cheeks like stars in the night before running down the lines of her smiling face and falling to the ground. Once Nana Ollie had disappeared through the gatehouse in the taxi, Tia opened her card to read the to-do list:

> Go on adventures,
> Learn new things,
> Love the people around you,
> Try to make the world a better place,
> And remember that you are wonderfully made.

Pasco had visited his grandmother for Christmas with his mother and younger twin sisters, and Tia was knocking on their door just a couple of hours after the Penrose family arrived back in Stormhaven. After a brief catch-up with Mrs Penrose downstairs, Tia headed up to Pasco's room to relay, in a hushed voice, the story of their encounter with Monsieur Moreau and everything her mother had told her on Boxing Day.

Tia had expected Pasco to look shocked or worried as

41

she told her tale. She was sure he would not have been keen to follow a suspicious character into a building that most people were leaving due to a blaring fire alarm, but he simply looked thoughtful. *Perhaps our search for the Thirteen Treasures of Britain toughened him up a little,* she thought.

"I wonder why that Frenchman was interested in seeing what the record said," he mused. "Maybe he has another clue about what happened to the black marble tomb and just wanted to check the Coron Arthur really was in there." After a pause, Pasco looked knowingly at Tia. "You think this is one of the Hallows of Arthur that Sanddef said we needed to find, don't you?"

She loved it when Pasco said "we" and included himself in the task. Though he was certainly curious, he was not naturally adventurous, and she knew it was only his loyalty to her that made him share the burden of this quest. "All we really know about the Hallows of Arthur is that they're items linked to him," she said.

"We've got 'stone, oak, circle', too." Pasco had spent the past month trying to work out what this cryptic clue meant. He was convinced that it pointed to some ancient site, but there were various stone circles and ancient circular wooden monuments across Britain that were possible candidates, and he could not think of a way to narrow the search.

"That hasn't really got us anywhere so far, though, has it?" Tia said.

"No," admitted Pasco. "Okay, let's find out what we can about the Coron Arthur."

"I wonder if there's anything else people thought of as belonging to King Arthur. Maybe there's a sword that everyone believed was the real Excalibur."

Pasco raised his eyebrows, clearly thinking they were clutching at straws.

But Tia persisted. "You're the one who once told me that 'Legends may be born from half-forgotten memory, or half-understood experience, but they're never just made up!'"

"O-kaaaaay." Pasco still didn't seem entirely convinced, but his faithfulness was greater than his doubt.

The two friends had little chance to do much research together over the next few days as the whole Penrose household came down with a virus that kept them virtually bedridden. Tia walked to Pasco's home a couple of times to deliver meals her mother had prepared for the family, but it was always Pasco's mother Endelyn who answered the door, and she thought it best that Tia didn't come in, just in case she caught the bug herself. Mrs Penrose also held a handkerchief over her mouth when she spoke to Tia, which made it tricky to understand what she was saying.

So Tia was left to find out what she could on her own, feeling all the time that Pasco was infinitely better at that sort of thing. She tried looking through the books on her parents' bookshelves in the sitting room and searching the internet, but she didn't get very far.

She found out about the Round Table and the knights questing for the Holy Grail, but this sounded more like the Norman King Arthur than the Celtic 'leader of battles' Arthur, whom Tia felt she had come to know.

Legends are never made up out of nothing, though, she reassured herself.

It felt as though Tia had been here before. Just a couple of months ago she had harboured doubts over the truth of the Thirteen Treasures of Britain; doubts that had gnawed away at her newly developing sense of who she was. And yet those treasures had turned out to be even more real and magical than she had ever imagined.

Perhaps she *could* entrust a little hope to the Coron Arthur and some of these other legends.

Chapter Eight

The Mysterious Death of Geoffrey Hemyke

On New Year's Day, the Trevelyans set off for Aberystwyth, on the west coast of Wales. Mr Trevelyan's archaeology conference was starting the following day, but the whole family was to make the trip in the hope of discovering more about Professor Hemyke: the murdered expert in ancient British legends who had lived and worked there, and with whom Tia had unknowingly shared a surname before becoming a Trevelyan.

As they drove under the portcullis and out of Stormhaven Castle in their little purple car, Tia had a sense of leaving her thoughts of the Coron Arthur in the courtyard car park and collecting a completely different set of mixed-up anxieties during the long journey into and across Wales.

She felt driven by a need to learn more about her birth story, yet she feared what she might discover. Her mind pitched from left to right and back again between different ideas of what might await her until she ended up with a motion sickness that had nothing to do with the way the car was weaving through the hilly Welsh countryside.

It was late afternoon by the time they arrived at the bed and breakfast where they would be staying for three nights, which was just a few minutes' walk from the Aberystwyth seafront.

"It's a little way from the university and national library," said Mr Trevelyan as they unloaded the car in the narrow street, "but it's very near to where Hemyke lived."

The building they were staying in was a large, ancient-looking, double-fronted house. Downstairs was a dining room for guests to have breakfast, with the private rooms of Mrs Gordon, the elderly widow who ran the establishment, at the back. Upstairs were a couple of guest bedrooms – one for Meghan and Tia, and one for their parents – and a bathroom. The top floor housed a couple of long-term residents in bedsits.

With Meghan having decided that her father could do with her help checking in downstairs, Tia found herself alone in the girls' room. She was sitting on her bed trying to settle her stomach when her mother came in. Tia returned Mrs Trevelyan's smile weakly, feeling grateful for the hug her mother offered as she sat down next to her.

"How about a short stroll to get some fresh air this evening?" Mrs Trevelyan said softly. "We'll see if we can find somewhere to eat. You probably don't feel very hungry, but a little food might help."

Tia nodded.

"Tomorrow we can go to the national library after dropping your dad off at the university for his conference. I've arranged to meet with one of the curators I worked with in the past. Hopefully, he'll be able to help us. We should also be able to view some of the manuscripts Professor Hemyke was working on. And when your father's finished for the day we can all try to track down some of Hemyke's university colleagues."

Tia nodded again.

The fresh air did help that evening. Salty sea air always seemed to fill Tia's lungs with more oxygen than any breath taken further inland or indoors. She also managed to eat a small amount when the family sat down for dinner at a pub overlooking the sea, though Meghan gladly finished the meal off for her.

Tia even managed to sleep relatively peacefully. When she woke to the sound of gulls and the sight of soft, wintry sunshine streaming in through the window, she felt the tiniest seed of hope nestled among the churning doubt.

"Gwen! How wonderful to see you again!"

The silver-haired curator Tia's mother had arranged to meet at the National Library of Wales was called Dr Ashforth. He was rather thin and wore thick glasses and a dusty green jacket that was slightly too big for him. The jacket had worn elbows, which Tia presumed came from resting them on tables as he pored over equally dusty old books all day. Tia and Meghan exchanged bemused looks as their mother and Dr Ashforth used a lot of impressive-sounding Welsh names that made absolutely no sense to them to update one another on what each was currently researching.

"And these are my daughters, Meghan and Tia," said Mrs Trevelyan, gesturing towards them. "In fact, Tia's the reason we've come today." She paused for a moment before continuing. "Before she took the name Trevelyan, Tia's surname was Hemyke."

Her tone was casual, and Dr Ashforth had been grinning broadly at the girls right up until he heard that last word. The smile vanished in an instant, as did all the colour from his face.

"*Hemyke?*" he whispered, an expression of disbelief on his face. "You're related to *Geoffrey* Hemyke?" He blinked as if to refocus. "He was a great scholar in our field, and his passing was deeply felt."

"The trouble is, Jonathan, we don't actually know whether Tia is related to Professor Hemyke or not." Mrs Trevelyan spoke gently but very seriously. "Tia was left on the doorstep of a children's home more than a hundred miles from here, and no one's ever been able to work out where she came from. The authorities never made the link, but her name and certain other factors convinced us that there was a connection between Tia and Geoffrey Hemyke."

"What other factors?" Dr Ashforth asked with a frown.

Mrs Trevelyan glanced briefly at Tia, then seemed to think better of mentioning too many details. "I just meant the timing of Hemyke's death and Tia's turning up at the children's home. But Hemyke's not exactly a common name. It couldn't just be a coincidence."

"Perhaps not, but I fail to see how I can be of help." He spoke as if this were a closing statement and stiffened up, looking decidedly nervous.

"We just want to know a bit more about what he was working on shortly before he died," Tia's mother said imploringly.

"I have no idea," the curator replied a little curtly. "But I know there were those who doubted his sanity towards the end."

Tia felt as though they were about to frighten him off, so she decided to make a direct and emotional plea. "Please, Dr Ashforth." Tia was planning to fake some tears, but as she began speaking she found that her eyes welled up quite naturally. "You don't know what it's like not knowing where you come from or whether your birth parents are even alive. I just want a chance… just a *chance* to maybe learn something about who I am."

Tia could see wet eyes behind his thick glasses.

Dr Ashforth opened and closed his mouth a few times before finally managing, "I'm sorry", then walked hurriedly away through a door that said: 'Staff Only'.

Meghan wrapped an arm around Tia, and their mother embraced them both. They decided to go and look at some of the last books Professor Hemyke had written and edited, but the most recent works he appeared to have contributed to had been published two years before his death.

They were just about to concede defeat and head back to the car when Dr Ashforth reappeared at the end of the aisle. He glanced around, as if to check that no one was watching, then hurried towards them, opening a book he was carrying as he moved. Tia could see a piece of paper inside the book that looked as if it had some sort of list on it.

The curator spoke in a hushed voice. "I'm in direct breach of the Data Protection Act," he whispered, "but here's a printout of all the books, journals and manuscripts Geoffrey Hemyke used our services to view in the year leading up to his death. Come to this room as soon as we open in the morning," he continued hurriedly, pointing at a number he had written at the top of the page in pencil, "and the manuscripts on the list will be available for you to view."

"Thank you so much, Jonathan," Mrs Trevelyan said, giving Dr Ashforth's hand a squeeze as she took the paper and folded it away in her jacket pocket.

"Gwen…" the curator's voice dropped to an even lower level, and Meghan and Tia both went up on tiptoes to hear what was being said. "You need to be careful. Geoffrey Hemyke was murdered because of something he was working on. I don't see how any of it could be connected to your daughter, but whatever he was researching became an obsession towards the end. He spent every minute of the working day here, barely speaking to anyone, and I always had to ask him to leave at closing time. After that we wouldn't see him for a couple of days, then he'd come back even more obsessed. You could see the strain on his face. And then suddenly the police were here asking questions because he'd been found dead at his home in suspicious circumstances."

"Thank you, Jonathan," Mrs Trevelyan said reassuringly. "We knew there was much to be wary about, but we have reason to believe that the man responsible for the murder is no longer a threat."

Dr Ashforth sighed at this, as if he had been holding his breath, but he still didn't look entirely at ease.

Tia had a slightly sick feeling at the thought of Mr Silverman – the suspected murderer – being buried alive in the underground cavern where they met Sanddef, but she tried to shake it off. "Thank you, Dr Ashforth," Tia said with a faint smile.

"I sincerely hope that you find what you're looking for, young lady." He smiled at Tia, nodded at her mother and sister, then turned and hurried off back down the aisle of dusty books.

Chapter Nine

Arwen Tresco

After lunch they looked up a few of the journals from the list Dr Ashforth had given them, but they all thought the manuscripts were likely to give them the most insight into any secrets that may have led to Professor Hemyke discovering the hiding place of the Thirteen Treasures of Britain. Tia had felt encouraged by Dr Ashforth's eventual agreement to help, yet a nagging voice in her head insisted that they would probably get nothing from the manuscripts… except maybe more questions.

As they left the library in the afternoon to meet Mr Trevelyan, Meghan whispered to Tia that she had brought with her the special torch Monsieur Moreau had dropped. She was convinced this would show up some hidden clue in the manuscripts but had thought it best not to mention it to their mother after she had said at the Tower of London that it was best not to shine too much light on ancient manuscripts. "We'll have to arrange some sort of diversion once we're in the room tomorrow so she doesn't notice," she whispered with glee.

They arrived at Aberystwyth University just as Mr Trevelyan was leaving the conference's seminar rooms. When Mrs Trevelyan asked how his day had been, he didn't mention anything from the lectures or seminars, but talked very excitedly about his lunch break. Not only had the sandwiches been excellent, but he had also got chatting to someone who was to lead a special archaeological excavation later in the year, which Mr Trevelyan seemed very keen to be involved in. Once they had told him about their encounter with Dr Ashforth, however, he managed to refocus on the other reason they had come to Aberystwyth.

"Right, then," he said. "Let's track down some of Hemyke's old colleagues. Gwen, do you know where to go?"

"The Department of Welsh and Celtic Studies is this way," his wife replied, leading them away. They did not have any prearranged meetings, as they had done at the library. Instead, their tactic was to roam the corridors, knocking on the doors of a few of the professors who had worked alongside Geoffrey Hemyke. This approach received mixed reactions.

One gruff man with a large beard refused to let them inside his office, and repeated several times that he had told the police everything he knew and, funnily enough, hadn't saved up any fresh information for a family of tourists. A scrawny little professor had looked nervous simply opening his door, before squeaking in panic at the mention of the name Hemyke.

After this, they changed tack and decided not to mention the real reason for their visit straightaway, instead letting Mrs Trevelyan make small talk about old Welsh legends first. One woman, whose office they did gain access to, welcomed them warmly once Mrs Trevelyan had dropped the names of several mutual academic friends. However, she began visibly trembling once they got on to the subject of Professor Hemyke. Then she suddenly remembered an urgent appointment and apologetically grabbed her coat as she hurried through the door, leaving them to show themselves out of her office.

Another man seemed so startled once the Trevelyans started asking about Hemyke that he stood up and sat down again repeatedly, clearly desperate to escape but at a loss as to how to do so. They managed to glean from this man that Geoffrey Hemyke had been working in almost solitary confinement for the last year of his life on what he assumed to have been something to do with the Thirteen Treasures of Britain.

"Just about the only times I spoke to him were when

he came to ask me about the cauldron of Dyrnwch the Giant," he said, standing up once more and laughing nervously. "He wanted to talk about the similarities between the various magical cauldrons of Celtic legend. Our last discussion felt very odd, as if he were talking about a real artefact while I was talking about tales and traditions."

The Trevelyans had a couple more encounters with nervous academics who had nothing helpful to tell them. They were loitering in a corridor, deciding whether or not to call it a day, when a lady with blonde hair that flowed down to her waist walked around the corner carrying far more books than any health and safety officer would permit.

She stopped outside the door to an office they had not yet tried and promptly dropped three books from the top of the stack. Meghan leapt forward and picked them up for her.

"Are you going in here?" Meghan asked, opening the door.

"Oh, yes, thank you!" The woman tried unsuccessfully to peer at her young visitor around the remaining tower of books in her arms, craning her neck left and right as she spoke. "Could you pop those three on my desk for me?"

The rest of the family had stepped forward to help, but attempting to remove any books from the pile looked as though it might unsettle the delicate balance, so they stayed back. Meghan placed the books on the desk, then held the door open while the lady staggered in and dumped the rest of the books on top, two of which immediately slipped off onto the floor. Meghan peered at the name on the office door and then looked quizzically at the lady, whose cheeks were puffed out as she rearranged the glasses that had almost slipped off her nose.

"Are you related to Elowen Tresco from Stormhaven?" Meghan asked.

"Why, yes," the lady replied, looking a little startled. "Elowen is my older sister."

"She teaches me guitar," Meghan beamed. "She's amazing!"

Tia glanced at the office door and saw 'Dr Arwen Tresco' written on the outside. She glanced back at the lady, who was now warmly greeting her parents, and saw the likeness between her and the older Tresco sister, who always seemed to have a mystical air about her when she sang in chapel services. This sister seemed slightly less mystical, Tia thought, but perhaps that was because of the way she had staggered into the room, glasses askew and dropping books.

"What on earth brings you all the way to Aberystwyth?" Dr Tresco asked. "And to the Department of Welsh and Celtic Studies, of all places!"

Mr Trevelyan just about managed to mention his conference before Meghan jumped in and gave Arwen a breathless rundown of their search for information about Geoffrey Hemyke. Tia felt Mrs Trevelyan rest a hand on her shoulder, as if to console her in case Meghan was saying more than she was comfortable with, but Tia didn't mind. It may simply have been Dr Tresco's connection to Stormhaven, but something made Tia feel much more comfortable in this particular office than she had felt with any of the other academics. She was also encouraged by Arwen's apparent lack of fear at the mention of Professor Hemyke's name.

"Well, I'm not sure I can be much help," she said, beckoning everyone in and shutting the office door behind them. "I joined the faculty staff just two days before Professor Hemyke's death, and I never met him, I'm afraid. But I can tell you that everyone here was deeply affected by the incident."

"Please," begged Tia, "anything you can tell us might be helpful. No one's really told us anything so far."

Arwen looked out of the window, where the sun had already dipped below the horizon. They had spent such a long time knocking on doors and getting nowhere that Tia was desperate to at least make one friend within Hemyke's old university department before they left.

"It's getting late," Dr Arwen said after a thoughtful pause. "If you don't have any other plans, why don't you come back to my place for dinner? That way I can tell you what little I know."

Arwen Tresco lived in a tiny village about twenty minutes' drive from the university. Despite the short notice, she was able to conjure up a delicious meal of pasta with tomato sauce and fresh basil leaves, smothered in parmesan cheese, for the five of them. Tia and Meghan ate eagerly as Dr Arwen told them all she could about Geoffrey Hemyke.

"As soon as I started in the department, I had people warning me about a smartly dressed, smooth-talking man who'd been hanging around, trying to find out where Geoffrey Hemyke was and what he was working on. University security staff had been informed because everyone felt quite threatened by him, but when they reported the man to the police they realised they couldn't recall any actual threat the man had made."

Tia knew at once that the person in question was Mr Silverman, the man who had found and threatened her at Ms Davidson's children's home and later at the Chamber of the Thirteen Treasures of Britain.

"The police said to keep them updated," Arwen continued, "but there wasn't really anything they could do at that time. Then there was a break-in and Hemyke's office was ransacked. No one could tell if anything had been taken; he'd been so private that no one knew what had been inside his office in the first place. They tried contacting Professor Hemyke, and that was when he was found dead at his home. I don't think they were able to categorically say it was murder, but his death was certainly treated as suspicious.

"As I say, everyone was deeply affected, but it was a mood of fear rather than of mourning. I think he interacted so little with people towards the end that very few counted him as a friend. The general feeling was that he'd possibly gone slightly mad, got involved with some dangerous people and endangered everyone in the department by association."

"Did you hear anything about what he'd been working on?" Mr Trevelyan asked once he and Meghan had finished the washing up and they were all sitting beside the open fire with mugs of hot chocolate.

"We know it was something to do with the Thirteen Treasures of Britain," Meghan said, becoming a little overexcited and sloshing some of her drink down the front of her jumper. "One of the other professors said he'd been asking about a giant's cauldron."

"Well, I don't know anything about giants and treasure," Dr Tresco laughed, "but I think it was his obsession with those sorts of things that led others to question his sanity. There are other things I heard people say about his behaviour, though. Apparently, he talked to a lot of people from the Gorsedd of Bards.

Some considered this to be less-than-serious work, but the bardic traditions are a vital part of the Welsh identity. Personally, I believe a wealth of oral stories, songs and poetry has been handed down by the bards, yet is missing from the written manuscripts."

This was where Tia stopped following the conversation and exchanged confused glances with Meghan.

Arwen must have noticed their vacant expressions. "Sorry, girls. This is my area of interest, and I forget that most people don't often hear words like 'Gorsedd' and 'bards' in everyday life." She looked at the clock on the wall. "It's a bit late now, but why don't you stop by my office for lunch tomorrow and I'll tell you more?"

Chapter Ten

Long-Lost Words

Tia, Meghan and their mother were waiting outside the national library when it opened in the morning and soon found their way to the room Dr Ashforth had marked on the paper he had given them.

Before opening the door, Mrs Trevelyan paused and turned to her daughters. "Now, girls, I know we're excited about viewing these manuscripts, but we need to remember that they're hundreds of years old and very fragile. I want you to promise me you won't touch them."

Tia agreed, as did a reluctant Meghan after rolling her eyes and sighing heavily.

The room was quite gloomy inside. About a dozen of the most ancient-looking pieces of paper Tia had ever seen were laid out across two tables in the middle of the room. There was a dense air of mystery about the manuscripts, and Tia spent ten minutes just walking around and gazing at each one in turn.

However, it soon became clear that Mrs Trevelyan was the only person who could really be of any use in this situation. The girls found they had to squint just to make out the letters written on the papers. Even when they were able to make out a string of letters in a row, the words were completely unintelligible, as they were written in Welsh. Tia recognised a few of the names she knew from the list of the Thirteen Treasures in English, so she could tell this was the topic of most of the manuscripts, but that was as far as she got.

It was at this point that Meghan sidled up to Tia, winked and took out the Frenchman's special penlight. She glanced around to check that their mother was bent over a manuscript at the other table before subtly shining the light on the paper in front of them. The strange glow showed up marks all over the ancient page but none of them looked remotely like words, either in Welsh or in any other language.

Meghan let out a disappointed tut.

"Girls!"

The sisters jumped at the sound of their mother's voice and the torch dropped to the floor.

"Perhaps you two should go out and have a look for some of the other books on this list," suggested Mrs

Trevelyan. "I'll swap it for that!" She passed Dr Ashforth's list to Tia and held out her hand until Meghan handed over the little penlight she had swiftly retrieved from the floor. Their mother said no more but maintained her disapproving expression as the girls shuffled out of the room.

After an hour, Meghan and Tia had located all the books on the list, but none appeared as interesting as the manuscripts. Despite mostly being written in English, they still didn't seem to make a lot of sense. They gathered them together on a reading table for their mother to look at. Tia could see little connection to the Thirteen Treasures beyond the fact that they were all about ancient Celtic legends.

With a sigh that expressed boredom rather than disappointment, Tia suggested they head back to the room of manuscripts to see how their mother was getting on. They reached the door just as Mrs Trevelyan opened it.

"What did you find?" Meghan blurted out excitedly.

"Well, I think we can be a little more sure of things we only suspected before." Mrs Trevelyan started walking towards the library's exit as she spoke. "One of the documents states that Bardsey was not the true location of the Thirteen Treasures, which we know Hemyke was also aware of. Instead, it says that the secret of the location was entrusted to a bard who *lived* on Bardsey. It seems the secret of the tests was entrusted to another bard. I've written down their names and the places they were said to live, although at times it was hard to tell which was the name of a person and which was the name of a place."

"So Professor Hemyke must have discovered the secrets these people were protecting," Meghan thought aloud as they emerged into the chilly January air. "Do you think that's why he was contacting lots of bards, like Arwen said? What even *is* a bard, by the way?"

"Perhaps Dr Tresco can explain that better than me at lunchtime," Mrs Trevelyan said. She turned to Tia, placed a hand on her shoulder and said gently, "One of the other documents said the secret of the key to entering the treasure chamber was also entrusted to a specific bard, just like the secrets of the location and the tests."

"But *Tia* was the key," Meghan said, looking somewhat bewildered. "She opened the secret chamber just by touching the symbol in the church. How could someone have known about Tia hundreds of years before she was born? Oh! Maybe it was a secret prophecy that Professor Hemyke worked out!"

Meghan began bouncing up and down, but Mrs Trevelyan remained focused on her youngest daughter. "I don't know what this means, Tia dear, but it's more than we had before, isn't it?"

More questions, thought Tia.

"So if all this was written on the manuscripts, how come more people don't know about it?" Meghan asked.

"Well, it wasn't exactly easy to see with the naked eye." Mrs Trevelyan coughed self-consciously, pushed a lock of hair back behind her ear and reached into her pocket. "I think the batteries have run out," she said, handing the tiny penlight back to Meghan and turning away without looking either of her daughters in the eye.

Chapter Eleven

The Secrets of the Bards

"Now, the first thing to understand is that, in just about every culture in the world, word of mouth has been the main way of handing traditions and knowledge down from generation to generation for thousands of years."

Dr Arwen Tresco had managed to get hold of a platter of sandwiches intended for the archaeological conference Mr Trevelyan was attending, and Meghan, Tia and Mrs Trevelyan were sitting in her office tucking into them as she gave them an introduction to the bards.

"Until the last few hundred years," she continued after taking a bite out of a salmon and cucumber sandwich, "only a small portion of people would have been able to read and write at all. In most societies, there would have been a select number of professionals whose job it was to learn stories, songs and poetry from the previous generation and teach them to the next, as well as to compose new works that captured life in their own day. This is what the bards were to the people of Britain.

"Nowadays, the tradition is continued by the Gorsedd – which sort of means association – of Bards. I understand that Professor Hemyke made a few connections with members of the Gorsedd, though no one knows exactly what he was trying to find out from them."

Mrs Trevelyan had suggested that they did not tell Dr Tresco what they had learned from the manuscripts. Meghan was literally biting her lip to prevent herself from declaring that, from what they had discovered that morning, they now had a pretty good idea what Professor Hemyke had been trying to find out. Tia thought it best to say something before Meghan's self-control failed her.

"Ummm," she said slowly, swallowing the last mouthful of her egg and cress sandwich, as if the thought had only just occurred to her, "do you think he could have been trying to find out something to do with the Thirteen Treasures of Britain from someone in the Gorsedd of Bards? Something that had been passed down for centuries?"

"A secret that was never written down, but was just passed on from person to person!" Meghan added excitedly.

"It's very unlikely," Dr Tresco replied, shaking her head.

Tia felt a little deflated but tried not to let it show.

"The modern Gorsedd was only founded during the eighteenth century," Dr Tresco continued. "That was about five hundred years after virtually all the bards were hunted down by Edward I after conquering Wales. A lot of work was carried out by non-bards and compiled in written form, but the rest of the oral tradition seems to have been lost for good during this five-hundred-year gap. So it may be that there were many more songs and stories from the bards that had been passed down by word of mouth for hundreds of years, but Edward I seems to have put an end to that centuries ago. There were sporadic gatherings of bards, but nothing very organised for five hundred years until the Gorsedd was formed."

She paused and looked dreamily out of the window. "At least, that's what the history books tell us. I suppose if individuals had information they considered to be critical – something about treasures of national importance – they would have done everything they could to ensure that this knowledge didn't die with them. They would have made sure it was passed on, even as their land was conquered." She blinked, turned back to Tia and Meghan, and smiled. "But now we're beginning to talk about these legends of treasure as if they're real, and everyone in this department thought

Geoffrey Hemyke was losing his sanity when *he* started talking like that!"

Tia and Meghan shared a knowing look with their mother as Dr Tresco selected a thick ploughman's sandwich with cheese and pickle.

Once Mr Trevelyan's conference had finished later that afternoon, the family found a small Indian restaurant in town. Meghan was able to relay the essential bits they had discovered during the day to her father before they had even walked through the door, though he needed his wife to explain a few things in a little more detail before he was able to understand what his daughter had told him.

"Well," he said after the family had ordered their main meals and begun tucking into the complimentary poppadoms and dips, "Arwen Tresco may think it unlikely, but the bards must have passed on secrets about the Thirteen Treasures through the centuries. Hemyke must have discovered everything he knew from somewhere: about the location of the hidden chamber, the tests you had to get past and the key to open the secret entrance in the first place," he added, grinning proudly at Tia, "because he found Tia and the gwyddbwyll pieces and wrote down the co-ordinates for the entrance to the chamber in Kirkburn. He must have discovered it from living bards because we know that's the line of investigation he was following."

"It's not that clear, though, is it?" Tia said quietly. Something had been niggling at her, and she felt it was time to voice it.

Her family looked at her quizzically, waiting for her to continue.

"The reason we've always thought there was a link to Professor Hemyke was because of my name. But Meghan worked out that I was only named Tia Hemyke because it's an anagram of 'I am the key'. Anyone could have given me that name. All this stuff we're finding out about Professor Hemyke is very interesting, but the link to me might just be a coincidence."

Mr Trevelyan started to say something but then stopped and looked very thoughtful. Mrs Trevelyan was staring at Tia, looking as if she might cry, and Meghan was frowning at the tablecloth, lost in open-mouthed contemplation. Clearly, none of them had considered this.

Their meals arrived and they began eating, but without the enthusiasm with which they had devoured the poppadoms. They ate in silence for a few minutes, nobody wanting to interrupt anyone else's thoughts.

Eventually, Mr Trevelyan spoke again. "You're right, Tia. We don't know who took you to Ms Davidson's, but maybe *who* isn't the most important thing. Whoever it was, they were undoubtedly trying to protect you, and they must have had *something* to do with Hemyke and his quest to uncover the bards' secret knowledge of the Thirteen Treasures. It would be too much of a coincidence for them not to."

"That's right," Meghan chipped in. "They could have called you Amy Keithe or Katie Hyme if they just wanted an anagram of 'I am the key', but they chose to use the name Hemyke. It must have been so they could link you to him."

Tia wondered for a moment whether Meghan had worked these other anagrams out earlier or on the spot. Tia was coming to realise that her sister's mind often moved as frantically as her body, and it would not have surprised Tia if Meghan had been scrambling the letters in her head even as she spoke. Judging by her parents' slightly stunned expressions, they were also taken aback by Meghan's impressive if somewhat random train of thought.

Her mother soon regathered her thoughts. "I know there are still a lot of unanswered questions," she said, gazing at Tia, "but we know more than we did when we first arrived, and there may be more we can find out about the bards. We know from the hidden writing on those manuscripts at the national library that one of them was entrusted with the secret of 'the key', and we know that refers to you."

"There's one more line of enquiry we can pursue before we leave tomorrow," Mr Trevelyan said. "We haven't yet seen if there's anything we can find out from Geoffrey Hemyke's former home."

"Do you know exactly where it is?" asked Tia.

"Yes," he replied, "and I think we'll be able to have a chat with Professor Hemyke's landlady, a certain Mrs Gordon, tomorrow."

It took Tia a while to recall who Mrs Gordon was, but then everything clicked into place.

"You mean…" began Meghan.

"Yes," Mr Trevelyan said, smiling mischievously. "Geoffrey Hemyke lived in one of the rooms in the very house we're staying in!"

Chapter Twelve

The Landlady's Tale

The Trevelyans did not see Mrs Gordon that evening, but Mr Trevelyan had made it clear that he wanted to wait until their final morning anyway, just in case their questioning spooked the landlady. It had upset so many people at the university that he was worried she might ask them to leave straightaway.

When they rose in the morning, their parents told the girls that they were to have breakfast before talking to Mrs Gordon about Geoffrey Hemyke, and that they should pack their things in advance.

Meghan felt exasperated that they were not able to get on with the interview straightaway and speedily stuffed all her belongings into her rucksack. Tia packed a little more thoughtfully, but both girls were packed and ready to leave the room within five minutes of receiving their parents' instructions.

Once downstairs, Meghan started shovelling her breakfast into her mouth as quickly as she had stuffed the clothes into her bag. Her mother had to beg her to slow down in case she choked. Tia experienced the familiar stomach twists of apprehension and anxiety that came with possibly discovering new truths but most likely being left with more questions. The prospect of subsequently returning to Stormhaven gave her comfort, however, and she was able to eat some of her breakfast.

"Is there anything else you need before you get going?" Mrs Gordon asked as she cleared the table and Mr and Mrs Trevelyan sipped the last of their coffee.

"Yes!" Meghan almost shouted in her excitement, instantly looking embarrassed. "Sorry," she said more quietly. "Yes, please."

"Not to worry, dearie." The landlady had looked startled by Meghan's outburst for a brief moment but her smile quickly returned. "What can I get you?"

"Actually," said Mr Trevelyan, "we were hoping you might be able to give us some information."

A strange sense of peace came over Tia at her father's words, as if it had merely been waiting for the conversation to start that had made her feel sick. Now it had begun, the churning ceased and she found herself taking over from her father, speaking to the old lady in a perfectly calm and steady voice.

"You see, Mrs Gordon, I was left on the doorstep of a children's home ten years ago with nothing to identify where I had come from except my name on a luggage label. We know that a man with the same surname lived here in Aberystwyth and died at almost the exact same time. In fact, he used to live in this very house."

Mrs Gordon's expression had gradually changed from a smile to one of open-mouthed shock. Meghan sprang up so the old lady could take her chair, as she looked as if she were about to faint. But despite dropping into it, the old lady's gaze never shifted from Tia's until she had finished with the words, "The name on my luggage label was Tia Hemyke."

Mrs Gordon took a deep breath and blinked some tears away from her eyes. She was unable to speak for some time, the words catching in her throat every time she opened her mouth. "I had no idea there was a child involved," she said at last. "What relation are you to him? I didn't know he had any children, never mind *grand*children."

"We don't actually know whether Tia is related to him," Mr Trevelyan said. "All we have is a name and various other factors that seem to connect them."

"What other factors?" the landlady asked, just as Dr Ashforth had two days before.

"There..." Mr Trevelyan paused before continuing,

"there was a man who came looking for Tia last year who we think also intimidated staff at the university, trying to find out what Professor Hemyke had been working on."

"A tall, unnecessarily well-dressed man with a slimy voice?" Mrs Gordon asked, wrinkling up her nose. "He came round here too, just before Geoffrey died, but Professor Hemyke had asked me not to let him in. One evening I came home to find the slimy chap walking down the stairs. He just smiled at me and let himself out. I went straight up to see if Geoffrey was all right. Shaking like a leaf in the breeze, he was, though he hadn't been hurt or even threatened outright, as far as I could tell. But then, he didn't tell me much at all."

"Staff at the university and the library told us Professor Hemyke became very obsessive about his work towards the end," Mr Trevelyan continued. "They said he seemed to be making long journeys and disappearing for a few days at a time. Do you know where he was going?"

"No, though I got the impression he went to a few different places, and he'd often be away for a night or two. He headed off soon after that visit from the man in the suit, and he looked so nervous before he left that I really pressed him to tell me where he was going, but he wouldn't. He just kept mumbling something about a key and keeping it safe. I feared for him that night, and I guess I was right to, because he was dead on the floor of his room the next time I saw him."

Tia swallowed. Professor Hemyke had become much more real to her over the last couple of days. Now his death suddenly felt more real.

"Do you know if he was in correspondence with anyone at this time?" Mrs Trevelyan asked.

"I think it was probably me he had most interaction with. I didn't realise how reclusive he'd been with the others at the university until the investigations after his death began. I never saw him talk to anyone, though he did send letters to people. He asked me to post a few for him. They were always addressed to people with titles like 'the Bard of Nefyn'. The police could never trace any of these people, and I think they may have just been the crazy notions of a man who was losing touch with reality. I'm sorry, I just don't think there's anything useful I can tell you. I told the others the same thing."

"*Others?*" Meghan asked, leaning in with interest.

"Yes, about six months after Geoffrey died, when the police had more or less closed the case without really solving anything, a man came knocking on the door asking whether I'd ever seen the professor in possession of a small pouch of silver coins and whether I recognised some strange symbol. He drew it on a piece of paper; it looked like two links of a chain squashed into a sort of X shape."

All four members of the Trevelyan family sat up a little straighter and exchanged knowing glances at the mention of what could only be Tia's little bag of treasures and the Solomon's knot symbol. Tia's hand rose to touch the pendant she still wore around her neck, tracing the familiar symbol with her fingers.

"And had you seen either of those things?" Mrs Trevelyan asked.

"Geoffrey was jingling a sort of old-fashioned coin bag absent-mindedly while he mumbled about keeping the key safe the night he set off on that last trip, but I've no idea whether there were any silver coins inside it. And I'd seen that symbol on the envelope of each letter he'd asked me to drop off at the post office for him. I told the man as much."

"What was he like, this man?"

"Very ordinary looking, really. About thirty, maybe. Glasses, brown hair. Most memorable thing about him was that he was carrying a guitar. He thanked me for the information and headed off."

"And there was more than one person who asked?" enquired Mr Trevelyan.

"Yes, the other one was very strange, though. About three years ago I received a letter written by a Lady Hendford from somewhere in Somerset, saying she would pay me well if I sent her any documents or other items Professor Hemyke had left behind. I replied, saying that the police had taken everything, so I couldn't help her."

"Do you have any details for either of these people?"

"You know, I think I might. I stuff all sorts of things

into my address book and hardly ever take anything out." She stood and hurried out of the room.

"These might not be the sort of people we want to be making contact with, Tom," said Mrs Trevelyan in a soft whisper while they waited for Mrs Gordon to return.

"I know," he whispered in reply, "but let's just gather all the information we can. We can think about what to do with it later."

"Here we are." Mrs Gordan re-entered the room with two pieces of paper in her hands. "You can have the letter Lady Hendford sent me. It's written on some fancy headed paper with her address at the top. And the chap who came to the door wrote his name and phone number down here in case I recalled anything else about the symbol and the silver coins. I hope they can help you." She smiled at Tia as she said this.

Tia smiled back.

It felt a little like their investigations at the library and the university; they had a couple of fresh leads but not a great deal of new knowledge. And yet Tia felt as though she understood her history slightly better. Simply encountering real people and places touched by Geoffrey Hemyke had somehow made the whole story seem more real. She felt she couldn't handle much more, however, and was blissfully happy when they got into the car a few minutes later to head home to Stormhaven.

Meghan wanted to talk about all her ideas. "I bet the

man who knocked on the door was one of the bards who knew the secrets of the Thirteen Treasures and had been talking to Professor Hemyke. We should definitely call him, don't you think, Tia?"

Tia pretended she was falling asleep so she didn't have to talk, and after just a minute or two she was no longer pretending.

Chapter Thirteen

Machicolations and Murder Holes

After such a busy Christmas break, Tia felt quite relieved when school began again, even though Mr Teague was making them walk along the castle battlements on a bitterly cold January morning. It hadn't felt too windy as they walked along the causeway and across the courtyard, but up at the top there was nothing sheltering them from the wintery winds charging at them from the sea. Most of the class were complaining in varying degrees, and others were suffering in silence with their hands buried in their pockets, but Tia was happily wrapped in a thick coat and an elaborate, multicoloured scarf Meghan had knitted for her as a Christmas present.

"I realised soon after I started knitting that it was going to be quite thin," Meghan had told her as she unwrapped it on Christmas morning. "So I made it extra-long to make up for it."

It had ended up being twice as long as Tia was tall, and Ivor Jones had teased Meghan about it non-stop, but Tia loved it purely for the devotion her sister had poured into crafting it. So far she had been able to say enough nice things to quell Meghan's temper, which had been rising steadily in line with Ivor's taunts.

"Right, everybody, this is your first task of the new term." Judging by the excited look on his rosy face, Mr Teague didn't mind the cold. He had what appeared to be a home-knitted scarf wrapped around his own neck, though his looked to have been made by a somewhat more experienced knitter.

Tia wondered if it had been a Christmas present from Miss Williams, the nursery teacher. Their blossoming romance had been the big piece of school gossip just before Christmas, when everyone – or at least most of the girls in Tia's class – had begun swapping tales about the various places Mr Teague and Miss Williams had been spotted together.

"I want you to go around the battlements looking for as many different defensive elements of the castle as you can," Mr Teague challenged the class. "Imagine being an archer defending the ramparts. What things about the building would help you? Imagine being a soldier besieging this fortress. What would hinder you from conquering the enemy? Use your imagination as well as your knowledge."

"Can I use your imagination?" Pasco said quietly as he shuffled up to Tia. "Mine doesn't work very well at the best of times, but it's got no chance of getting warmed up in this cold."

"As long as I can use all your knowledge," Tia replied, grinning at her friend.

The two set off but talked little of castles at first. Instead, Tia updated Pasco on what the Trevelyans had found out during their time in Aberystwyth.

"So Hemyke found out about the bards' secrets from the manuscripts," Pasco began summarising after a thoughtful pause. "Then he tracked down the modern-day bards, who had become the keepers of the secrets relating to the Thirteen Treasures. He found the gwyddbwyll pieces and the location of the treasure chamber in Kirkburn, but Mr Silverman was after him. He found the key, *you*, probably from a bard again, and took you and the gwyddbwyll pieces to the children's home to protect you just before Mr Silverman murdered him."

"Yeah, that's what it looks like," Tia agreed. All the information had been sloshing around in her head, but she had been unable to draw such clear conclusions from it. Her thoughts always seemed to make more sense once Pasco had said them out loud.

"Those two people who were asking about him afterwards sound a bit odd," Pasco said with a frown. "Are you going to contact them?"

"Dad wants to call the man with the guitar. Oh, and guess what the name was that he wrote down with his phone number for Mrs Gordon. Brandubh!"

Brandubh was the name of an ancient Celtic board game that Tia and Pasco had come to know very well a few months earlier.

"That's weird!" Pasco laughed. "Do you know anything about the bards whose names your mum found on the manuscripts yet?"

"No," Tia answered. "She's done a bit of research since we got back, but she couldn't find anything. She said I should write to Arwen Tresco and ask her about them, because she can't think of anyone who knows more about the bards than Arwen does. But she said I'm not to tell her how we came across them. I think she's a bit ashamed of herself for using the penlight after telling Meghan off for using it!"

"I might tell my mum she should try it out on some of the old documents in the library here," Pasco said, only half joking. "There are probably loads of secrets in there."

"I've already written the letter," Tia said, "and I

asked if she knows any bard stories about the Hallows of Arthur, but I kept that bit a secret."

After her underground adventures in the Chamber of the Thirteen Treasures, and Tia's narrow escape from Mr Silverman, the Trevelyans had assumed that the dangerous aspects of her mysterious history were over. Tia had decided not to dampen their relief by telling them she had been given another potentially perilous quest by Sanddef.

"I didn't find any real artefacts that might be Arthur's on my own," she continued. "Did you find anything?"

"A bit, yeah." Pasco pushed his glasses back up his nose, then hastily put his hand back in his pocket to keep it warm. "In 1191, King Richard I gave the king of Sicily a sword that he claimed was Arthur's sword, Excalibur, though the legends say that Arthur ordered that Excalibur be given to the Lady of the Lake. In the old Welsh legends Arthur's sword was called 'Caledfwlch', which became 'Caliburn' in English and then eventually 'Excalibur'."

Slightly stunned by the depth of detail Pasco was able to recall, Tia also felt a little confused. "Who is the Lady of the Lake?" she asked.

"She's some sort of magical person who lived at the bottom of a lake and first gave Excalibur to Arthur. She's also the mother of the legendary knight Sir Lancelot. She's from the medieval legends rather than the ancient Welsh myths."

"Right." Tia already doubted that this would be a promising line of enquiry. "And where's Sicily?"

"It's an Italian island."

"I'm not sure I can arrange a trip over there any time soon," Tia sighed, "but I suspect King Richard just made up the idea that the sword he gave the King of Sicily was Excalibur, anyway. English kings seem to have liked using the legends of King Arthur to make themselves look good."

"Yeah, and lots of them tried to mimic the Round Table. Edward I had a Round Table made for feasting at Winchester, and Henry VIII had it repainted with the names of various Arthurian knights around it and a picture of himself as King Arthur! You can still see the top of the table hanging on the wall in Winchester's ancient Great Hall."

"Wow, you found out a lot!"

Pasco raised his eyebrows and scoffed, "Well, I had a lot of spare time while we were all ill after Christmas."

"Edward I again," Tia said thoughtfully. "He was a quite a King Arthur fan by the sound of it. You didn't find anything that could have been *the* Round Table, though?"

Tia looked hopeful, but Pasco shook his head. "There are a few sites across the country that look like they may have been meeting places where everyone sat in a large circle, but that's about it. And I couldn't find any actual reference to the Hallows of Arthur at all."

Tia was impressed, if a little intimidated, by Pasco's research skills. And yet, for all his hard work, they still didn't have any promising leads for tracking down the long-lost artefacts associated with King Arthur, apart from the Coron Arthur.

"Oh well," she said. "I'd still like to know more about Arthur's crown being kept at Glastonbury. Arwen Tresco might be able to tell us something about bardic legends concerning the Hallows of Arthur."

By now the two friends had walked halfway round the battlements and decided they should probably start completing the task Mr Teague had set them. They began by noting the slits in the walls that allowed archers to shoot out while making it very difficult for attackers to shoot back at them.

Tia remembered a large book on castles that she had spent hours hiding behind at Ms Davidson's house. It was full of labelled diagrams that she could still see vividly in her mind's eye. Recalling this now, she pointed out to Pasco how the wall on the outside of the castle battlements allowed archers to shoot over the lower parts while they sheltered behind the taller parts. He was extremely impressed when she explained that the taller parts were called 'merlons' and the gaps in between them were called 'crenels'.

Walking on, they noticed holes in the floor at the base of the rampart through which defenders could drop or fire things onto attackers outside the castle wall below. Pasco thought these were called 'murder holes', but he wasn't sure. He turned a light shade of red later in the classroom when it turned out he was wrong.

"Looks like I didn't contribute much imagination *or* knowledge today," he whispered to Tia after Mr Teague had pointed out the difference between machicolations – the holes that extended beyond the castle walls, which they had seen earlier – and murder holes – holes in the ceiling of arched gateways leading into castles.

"There isn't much difference between them, though," Tia said, trying to reassure him. "They're both holes for dropping things onto people."

"You should have just done the activity on your own," Pasco huffed. Tia looked at the sulking boy next to her and stifled a chuckle. Perhaps it was good for him to get something wrong every now and then.

Mr Teague was busy going through some photos Meghan and Bran had taken of different defensive castle features. He had given them the task of gathering photographic evidence, partly to distract Meghan before she lost her temper over Ivor's teasing about Tia's scarf, but also because he knew this was often the best way for them to learn. Paper and pencil sometimes proved to be an obstacle to their enthusiasm.

To their credit, they had done a very thorough job, even embellishing their photographs by taking it in turns to pose as medieval soldiers to demonstrate how each feature would have been used.

At the end of the day, Mr Teague announced that they would be doing a lot more work this term on military defences and how they had changed through the centuries. He then dismissed them, declaring that they had all worked exceptionally hard for their first day back.

The rest of the week was spent delving into medieval siege warfare. One particularly wet morning, Mr Teague split them into two groups so they could take it in turns to play the parts of attacking and defending soldiers by hurling tennis balls at each other: one group up on the battlements of the castle, the other down on the ground. The foul weather emphasised his point that it was much harder to fire upwards as an attacker than to fire downwards as a defender.

The defenders also dropped footballs onto the attackers through the machicolations. Roderick Payne later remarked that the threat of this football bombardment had made them stay back from the walls, which only served to make them easier targets for those throwing the tennis balls. Mr Teague beamed with pride at the insightful observation his student had made.

Then the classmates interviewed each other as attackers and defenders about their differing experiences of 'the Siege of Stormhaven Castle'. This led them to consider more effective methods attackers could employ, such as siege towers to take away the defenders' advantage of higher ground, and the long-term tactic of simply cutting off a castle's supply chains and starving the inhabitants out.

As the month progressed, the whole class became thoroughly engrossed in their medieval warfare studies. One clear, crisp January afternoon, Bran's father, Mr Corentyn, and two other experimental archaeologists accompanied the class to a large field just outside the castle wall for a practical demonstration of archery.

The adults fired arrows using an array of replica bows based on everything from the English longbow to a Mongol 'recurve' bow with its curled ends and an imposing-looking crossbow. The class compared the distances the different bows could shoot and calculated the average speeds of the arrows, using stopwatches to time each flight.

Then they experimented with angles of release to find out which gave the greatest distance. This activity lasted a while, because Bran chose angles such as 41.5 degrees and insisted that his father shoot precisely at the angle he had requested. Tia suspected Bran was feeling a little frustrated that they hadn't been allowed to use any of the bows themselves and was taking it out on his dad.

The following week they were finally allowed to have a turn at using smaller replica bows. Bran's dad took them out in groups of four, and Tia discovered that she had a real talent for archery. It was hard work pulling the bowstring back as far as she could, but Mr Corentyn lavished praise on Tia for her steady hand and calm release. At the end of the session he invited Tia to come and practise whenever she wanted to outside of school.

"You'll be on the county archery team within months," Mr Corentyn predicted, much to the annoyance of Gareth, Aled and Dafydd, the three older boys in Tia's group.

Chapter Fourteen

A Letter Arrives

Early in February, Tia asked her parents whether they had contacted either of the people Mrs Gordan had told them about who had gone looking for Professor Hemyke. It was a Friday evening and Meghan was out at a guitar lesson with Elowen Tresco.

Tia seemed to have the most important conversations with her parents on the nights when her sister was out. It wasn't that she didn't want Meghan to know what they told her – she kept Meghan almost as up-to-date as she did Pasco – it was just that they were less likely to go off on a tangent when her sister wasn't around to distract them.

Mrs Trevelyan was cooking dinner and Mr Trevelyan

was sitting at the kitchen table trying to fix the toaster. He had managed to take it apart quite quickly but seemed unsure how to put it back together.

"Well, we found out a bit about Lady Hilary Hendford and decided it might be best *not* to contact her," Mrs Trevelyan answered.

"She's a keen collector of all sorts of antiquities," Mr Trevelyan explained, "but there are doubts over whether her methods of collecting them are entirely legal. Although nothing has ever actually been proven and she's never been charged with anything."

Tia had a vivid flashback to a comment Mr Silverman had made in the Chamber of the Thirteen Treasures about 'her Ladyship' not being pleased if anything were damaged. She wondered if there was any connection.

"And what about the man with the guitar – Brandubh?" Tia asked.

"I'm still on his trail," her father answered, frowning at a coiled spring he was holding in his fingers, apparently clueless as to how to fit it back inside the dismembered toaster. "The number he left was for a pub in a little village just outside Cardiff. The landlord there said Brandubh passed through every so often and usually played a few gigs, but that he hadn't seen or heard from him in a couple of years.

"He gave me the names of a few other pubs where he sometimes played, but when I looked them up, they said more or less the same thing, each one giving me a few more pubs to look up. And that's how it seems to be continuing. No one's seen or heard from him in a while, but everyone knows of a few places he might be. So I've got an ever-growing number of potential leads to work my way through."

It wasn't exactly promising, but Mr Trevelyan didn't sound as though he intended to give up any time soon. He was still puzzling over the entrails of the toaster, and Tia smiled quietly at his honest dedication to every cause.

At that moment, Meghan flung open the front door excitedly. "Tia!" She burst into the kitchen waving an envelope. "I've got a letter for you!" She briefly glanced at her father and the pieces of toaster strewn across the dinner table. "No toast for breakfast in the morning, then," she said before returning her attention to her sister. "It came with a letter Elowen Tresco received. It's from Arwen!"

Tia took the envelope but was hesitant to open it in the kitchen. She was concerned that if her parents saw any mention of the Hallows of Arthur they might start asking awkward questions and she wanted to keep the quest for the Hallows a secret for now. She was thankful when her mother announced that dinner was almost ready and asked the girls to help Mr Trevelyan clear the table of toaster fragments.

Meghan couldn't begin to fathom how Tia was able to wait, gazing open-mouthed as she simply stuffed the envelope into her pocket to read later. It wasn't until their father started talking about a potential summer camping trip that Meghan was finally distracted.

"I got talking to a marine archaeologist from Southampton at the conference in Aberystwyth," Mr Trevelyan began. "He told me about a project they're undertaking at Bala Lake in North Wales later in the year. After I told him about my underwater experience, he invited me to become part of the team."

"What underwater experience?" Tia asked, a little perplexed. She sometimes forgot she had only been a Trevelyan for about five months, and from time to time she would happen upon a whole chapter of her parents' lives that she knew nothing about.

"Your Nana Ollie's love for exploring the seas and looking for clues to maritime mysteries isn't anything new," Mr Trevelyan explained. "Your uncles and I were pretty much raised on the ocean. I think I spent more time on boats than I did on land as a child, and I learned to scuba-dive as soon as I was big enough to carry an air tank on my back. Sailing around the coast in search of sunken treasure is how I first got into archaeology, though it's been a long time since I last did any proper marine excavation. So I got very excited when I heard about this. I'd have to spend virtually the whole summer holiday in Bala, but we could all camp there. I'm sure you girls would have loads to do: kayaking, canyoning… and I think you can do caving near there, too."

Meghan was sold, though she made it clear that she wanted to be involved in the underwater exploration as well. Her father explained that the girls were probably too young to scuba-dive, but he would certainly find ways they could help.

Meghan began to protest, but Tia's thoughts had already returned to the letter in her pocket. She imagined what information it might hold, and whether she might, for once, find more answers than questions.

Chapter Fifteen

What the Letter Said

Alone in her room later that evening, Tia opened the envelope and removed two folded pieces of paper. She flattened them out and began to read:

Dear Tia,

It was lovely to hear from you so soon after your visit, and I was eager to try to help you out. I'm afraid I haven't been able to find out very much, but I hope what I have discovered will be of interest to you.

Tia had to reread the next few paragraphs several times; first to check whether it was written in English or

Welsh, and then to wade through Arwen's wordy way of expressing herself, giving far more information than was necessary. It seemed to be a long list of Welsh bards and place names, with long-winded explanations of how one name might be linked to some other place or person.

When she finally got to the end of the first page, she realised Arwen had finished her explanation with a much more understandable summary:

> So, to cut a long story short, it looks to me as if all the names of those people and places might just be indicating one place, the island of Bardsey, and the two most famous ancient Welsh bards, Aneirin and Taliesin.

Sighing with relief at finally being able to understand something, Tia put the first page aside and turned to the second part of Arwen's letter:

> Your question about the Hallows of Arthur really intrigued me, as I had never heard this phrase before. I did a lot of digging and eventually found one reference made by an unnamed eighteenth-century English gentleman who recorded a conversation he fell into with an old Welsh man at an inn while travelling through rural mid-Wales. He says that the old man called himself a bard from the Order of Myrddin and spoke of a legend, known as the Hallows of Arthur, as described in this cryptic poem:

Where Arthur held court, his men around him,
Where Arthur rests, and that which armed him,
That which covered his head to crown him,
That which enfolded that none might harm him.

I have never heard of a bardic Order of Myrddin, but
Myrddin is an early British poet, about whom it is
especially difficult to separate fact from myth. He was
undoubtedly a historical person, but he morphed into the
legendary person of Merlin centuries ago, and it is very
difficult to distil historical fact from everything that has
been written about him.

Taliesin is also shrouded in myth, though not quite to
the same extent. Like Myrddin, some legends have him as
a member of King Arthur's court, and there is a poem
attributed to him in which he is part of an expedition led by
Arthur to retrieve a cauldron from the underworld.

I'm sorry not to have been able to find out more than this,
and I'm afraid that what I have found is little more than
obscure literary curiosity, but hopefully it's of some interest
to you. Let me know if I can help you with anything else.
If any of what I have written is confusing, I'm sure your
mother will be able to explain it better than I have. She is
an excellent historian of sub-Roman Britain and will be

familiar with Aneirin, Taliesin and Myrddin.

I do hope to be able to see you again soon. I'm long overdue a visit to see Elowen in Stormhaven and am thinking of coming down at Easter.

Yours,

Arwen

The Hallows of Arthur poem had given Tia goosebumps. She decided that "where Arthur held court, his men around him" must be a reference to the Round Table. *Could "where Arthur rests" be a reference to Arthur's grave?* she wondered. *Or isn't there a legend about Arthur being taken to the Isle of Avalon rather than dying? "That which armed him" must be Excalibur,* she figured, *and "that which covered his head to crown him" has to be his crown, the Coron Arthur.* Finally, Tia assumed "that which enfolded that none might harm him" must be the cloak, which she already had.

Tia had no idea how to start looking for the Round Table, Excalibur or Avalon, but she was convinced that Glastonbury Abbey was the place to start looking for the Coron Arthur, which was beginning to call to her the way the Thirteen Treasures had.

Aneirin and Taliesin also sounded important. Tia decided to take Arwen's advice and ask her mother about them, but she didn't want to show her the whole letter. The night she and Pasco had escaped from the Chamber of the Thirteen Treasures, Tia had decided to keep the quest for the Hallows of Arthur a secret, maintaining the impression that the Thirteen Treasures had marked the end of the trail. As far as her parents were concerned, Tia's quest was purely to learn more about Professor Hemyke and find out how she came to be at Ms Davidson's children's home. Tia wanted to keep it that way because she knew they would try to stop her if they thought she was doing anything that might put her in danger.

She folded up the second half of the letter and tucked it between the pages of her journal.

"Aneirin!" her mother exclaimed the following morning when Tia showed her what Dr Tresco had written in the first half of her letter the next day. "Taliesin! Yes, of course!" She said the names as *An-air-rin* and *Ta-lee-ess-in*.

Mrs Trevelyan was sitting with a bowl of cereal positioned among the pieces of toaster that were once again spread across the kitchen table, Mr Trevelyan having continued to work on it after dinner the night before. She nodded to herself between spoonfuls as she pored over the piece of paper Tia had shown her.

"I don't quite know what to make of it, though," Mrs Trevelyan continued with a frown.

"Professor Hemyke must have worked something out after he found the names in the manuscripts," Meghan chipped in as she craned over her mother's shoulder.

"Is there a connection between these people and Arthur?" Tia asked, as if she didn't already know the answer.

"According to some legends, yes," her mother replied. "The Book of Taliesin includes a tale of Arthur leading a quest to the underworld that Taliesin took part in. But from a historical perspective, most of the evidence suggests that Taliesin lived a little later than the Arthurian battles."

"Even if he didn't actually hang out with King Arthur," Meghan said with gleaming eyes, "he could still have been a secret-keeper for the location of the Thirteen Treasures."

"I suppose he could," Mrs Trevelyan admitted, grinning instead at the awed way in which Meghan had said "secret-keeper". "Although," she added, looking thoughtful, "the manuscripts didn't say that Taliesin or Aneirin knew *where* the treasures were." She glanced between Arwen's letter and a page of notes she had made while inspecting the manuscripts in Aberystwyth. "The location of the chamber was known by the bard on Bardsey. It looks as if Aneirin was entrusted with the secret concerning the tests one had to pass to get to the chamber – presumably the gwyddbwyll pieces – and Taliesin was supposed to be the guardian of the *key* to the treasures."

Tia's mother and sister gazed at her, and she felt as though many more eyes – those belonging to centuries of nameless secret-keeping bards – were also looking at her. Tia wondered if this Taliesin person could have been charged with the task of guarding a secret that had something directly to do with her. She was separated from this person by almost fifteen hundred years. *What does it even mean that he was supposedly guarding the key if I am the key?*

Tia suddenly felt exhausted. Sensing this, Mrs Trevelyan put away her notes and asked Meghan to take a cup of tea up to Mr Trevelyan, who was still in bed, and to ask if he was planning to finish fixing the toaster right away. Tia was left alone with her thoughts, and she continued to stare at Arwen's letter for some time.

Chapter Sixteen

Dead Ends and Lost Paths

Pasco knocked on the Trevelyans' door after lunch that same Saturday. On her birthday three months earlier, Pasco had given Tia a copy of an ancient map of Stormhaven that had all sorts of paths as well as the island's standing stones marked on it. The drama of their Thirteen Treasures quest, their separate travels over Christmas and the New Year, and the wet, windy January weather had prevented the two friends from following any of the ancient trails until today. As eager as she was to learn more about her own mysterious history and pursue the Hallows of Arthur, Tia was looking forward to an afternoon spent exploring the island with her friend.

Before heading out, Tia took Pasco upstairs to show him the letter from Arwen Tresco.

"So the bard on Bardsey Island knew where the Thirteen Treasures were," he said after hearing Tia's account of what Mrs Trevelyan had told her. "Aneirin had the Gwith…" he slurred before gesturing towards the pendant around Tia's neck, "the silver pieces to pass the tests. And Taliesin knew something that somehow led directly to you."

"I didn't show Mum this bit because she doesn't know about the task Sanddef set me about the hallows." Tia handed Pasco the second page of Arwen's letter and smiled at how it had almost become normal to think of Mrs Trevelyan as Mum. *Almost.*

"Well, it's definitely the most promising piece of information that's turned up so far," Pasco said, handing the letter back to Tia after reading it. He picked up the map they would be using to find the ancient paths around the island and slid it into a plastic sleeve for protection.

Tia laid the letter down on her bed to finish packing her rucksack with a few things they might need that afternoon. She was feeling more positive about their search for the hallows than she had for a while. "And it's pretty clear what the hallows actually are," Tia added, popping a shiny, nautical-looking brass compass – a

Christmas present from Nana Ollie – into her bag. "Excalibur, the Round Table, Arthur's final resting place, the cloak – which we already have – and the coron, which we're at least on the trail of. It may even be connected to the grave of Arthur in Glastonbury, though nobody seems to think it's real."

Pasco looked doubtful. "It just doesn't feel as *old* as it did when we were finding out about the Thirteen Treasures, does it? It's like those things are more to do with the later medieval legends of King Arthur than old Welsh legends like the Thirteen Treasures. I mean, this old Welsh bard from the Order of Myrddin that Dr Tresco talked about was only alive about two or three hundred years ago."

Tia paused, holding a folded raincoat she was about to stuff inside her rucksack. "You reckon this legend might not be true?"

It suddenly seemed a bit hasty to pin any hopes on one isolated account from an unnamed person more than two hundred years ago.

"I'm not saying *that*," Pasco said hurriedly. He always seemed to panic when he thought he might have done something to upset Tia. "I just wonder if there might be a more cryptic explanation. I mean, 'that which enfolded that none might harm him' isn't the most obvious way to describe the Mantle of Arthur, is it? How could a mantle stop anyone harming him?"

Tia dropped the raincoat and knelt down to pull a

bundle of cloth out from under her bed. She unfolded the hooded cloak they had retrieved from the Chamber of the Thirteen Treasures and rubbed the fabric between her fingers. Pasco was right; it was just made of tightly woven wool. How could it protect anyone from harm?

"But it *was* supposed to make whoever put it on invisible, remember?" Tia exclaimed, feeling hopeful again.

"It didn't make you invisible when you tried it on in Kirkburn, did it? But this is the thing we're most sure is one of the hallows. So if this poem Dr Tresco told you about is real, the cloak has to fit in somewhere… which just makes me think we might not be reading the poem properly. Maybe the items the bard from the Order of Myrddin was talking about aren't as obvious as they seem… like the cloak."

"You mean Arthur might have held court around a square table instead of a round one?" Tia raised her eyebrows doubtfully, but she could see that Pasco was right about the cloak.

"There might not have been a table at all," he suggested.

Tia sighed and puffed out her cheeks, still rubbing the woollen fabric of Arthur's hooded cloak between her fingers. She wasn't quite sure where all this left them.

The thoughtful silence was broken by the sound of someone approaching on the landing.

"I've made a box of snacks for you to take with you."

Mrs Trevelyan's voice had filtered through from the other side of the door, but Tia knew she was about to enter the room. She instinctively stuffed the cloak into her rucksack, just managing to conceal it before her mother came in holding out a plastic tub that rattled with the sound of nuts and chocolate raisins.

Tia smiled as naturally as she could and took the box, racking her brain to recall where she had left Arwen's letter featuring the hallows poem and whether it was out of Mrs Trevelyan's view. "Thanks, Mum, we were just about to set off." Tia packed the snack box on top of the cloak, slung the rucksack over her shoulder and moved towards the door in an attempt to lead her mother away before she had a chance to spot the letter, wherever it happened to be.

"That was close," Tia whispered to Pasco once they were outside. "I couldn't remember what I'd done with the letter."

"It's here." Pasco held up the plastic wallet they'd put the map in to protect it from rain, flipping it over to show the letter slotted in behind it. "I put it in just before your mum opened the door. I didn't know what else to do with it – sorry."

Tia sighed with relief.

Having the poem with them meant they inevitably looked at and talked about what it could mean when they stopped to eat their snacks. The hike had been hard going, as all the ancient paths marked on the map appeared to have become completely overgrown over the past few centuries so that they were now non-existent. After spending most of the afternoon picking their way through bracken and gorse bushes, they had stopped for several breaks, discussing the hallows poem each time.

By the time they had sat down beside the third standing stone – all of which seemed to be as they were marked on the map – they had discussed the poem so extensively that Tia now knew it off by heart. Despite all their discussions, Tia and Pasco kept returning to the idea that the hallows had to be the Round Table, Excalibur, the cloak, Arthur's crown and wherever Arthur was laid to rest: either his grave or Avalon, where he was said to have been taken after suffering a mortal wound, and where he was still believed to be waiting until he was most needed.

"Our quest would be a whole lot easier if 'where Arthur sleeps' *was* just his grave at Glastonbury," Pasco said, chewing thoughtfully on a mouthful of peanuts. "Given that Avalon's a mythical island that lies between life and death, it sounds like it's going to be pretty hard to find."

Tia laughed but said nothing. The idea that Arthur was dead rather than just sleeping seemed a bit anticlimactic somehow, even if it would have made their quest easier. She could understand why many believed the discovery of Arthur's body to have been a Norman trick to squash the hopes of native Britons. The thought of him lying dormant somewhere, waiting to return in a blaze of glory, was inspiring. It somehow gave more purpose to her quest.

"Have you thought about why the hallows have to be gathered at all?" Tia had only started thinking about this in the last week or so. Before that she hadn't needed a reason to search for them; the fantastical way the task had been given to her was enough to spur her on. But as life had settled back into something like normality, she had begun to think about the ultimate aim of it all.

Pasco thought for a long time before answering, gazing at Tia all the while. "You think gathering them's going to bring Arthur back to life, don't you?"

"It seems the most likely outcome, doesn't it?"

Pasco laughed. "Our lives have become pretty weird if we think bringing a fifteen-hundred-year-old man back to life is *likely!*"

Tia laughed with him. It felt good to be sitting outside with her best friend and laughing together, even if the skies were becoming gloomier and the wind was picking up.

"Why would this be the time that Arthur's most needed, though?" Pasco mused after a while. "There have been Viking invasions, a Norman invasion, a civil war and two world wars since Arthur's day, and he didn't wake up for any of those, did he?"

"We haven't woken him up yet either, have we?" Tia said ominously. "Maybe there's some big disaster just around the corner that we don't even know about yet, and that's why we need Arthur."

"Or maybe it'll take us our whole lives to complete the quest and the danger's still sixty years away." Pasco flopped backwards in feigned exhaustion, lying out on the grass with his eyes shut.

"Will you still help me even if it takes sixty years?"

"Course I will!" Pasco answered without opening his eyes.

Tia grinned broadly to herself, then turned to see two people in the distance walking towards them. Still a little way off, they seemed completely unaware of Tia and Pasco.

"Is that Mr Teague?" she asked, squinting at the two approaching figures.

Pasco sat up and followed the direction of her gaze. "Yeah, and that's Miss Williams, my sisters' teacher. They love her."

"They're holding hands!" exclaimed Tia. "Should we say hello?"

"Er…" Pasco paused as the two adults, still oblivious to how close they were to Tia and Pasco, halted, turned to face one another and kissed. "No, I don't think we should say hello. That might be quite embarrassing for everyone." He blushed.

"They're going to walk right up to us, though,"

said Tia in a hushed voice, nodding her head towards the pair, who were still locked in a lingering embrace. "Assuming they stop doing that anytime soon and actually start walking again, that is."

"Quick!" gasped Pasco. "Into the bushes!"

They gathered up their bags as quickly as possible without making a noise before ducking into the bushes on the other side of the standing stone. They picked their way through the undergrowth, trying to avoid the thorniest plants. After a few minutes, they emerged onto another path close to the farthest edge of the island from the village. Here the terrain fell away steeply down towards the sea on one side, where the land had been pummelled by frothing waves. The sky was dark with threatening clouds, and Tia and Pasco suddenly felt exposed to the elements.

"That was close," Pasco panted. "It's this way back to the village from here, isn't it?"

Tia didn't appear to be listening. Her attention was focused in the opposite direction, her eyes fixed on another couple of individuals in the distance who appeared to be talking very seriously together as they walked in the direction of the castle keep and the causeway.

"Who's that?" Tia said, more to herself than to Pasco.

"They're not snogging as well, are they?" Pasco asked, squinting in the direction of Tia's gaze and looking worried again.

"No," Tia answered, still frowning at the two, who had just turned and were walking away from them. "I think they're plotting something. That's Llacheu Thunderford; Lord Reg's son who wants to turn the school into a hotel. I don't know who the other man is." It took Tia two seconds to decide what to do next. "Come on, let's follow them."

"But it's going to rain," whined Pasco, looking up at the clouds, then eyeing the huge drop down to the crashing sea.

"So put your raincoat on." Tia had already set off in pursuit of the conspirators. "If he's making plans to shut down the school, I want to know about it."

Pasco hurried along after her, struggling with his raincoat and rucksack. Having started to drizzle just seconds earlier, it was beginning to rain quite hard and Tia was getting wet. She reluctantly stopped to take her raincoat out of her bag, only to discover it wasn't there.

"Mum came in just as I was packing my coat, and I put Arthur's cloak in instead," she groaned. "Oh well." She pulled the Mantle of Arthur out of her bag while Pasco waited a few paces in front of her. "Keep an eye on those two so we don't lose them," she said, opening the hooded cloak out to its full size.

It was an adult's cloak, and Tia was small for her age, so it took a bit of effort to get it positioned round her shoulders, and quite a lot of it was dragging on the floor. Had her thoughts not been so preoccupied with following Llacheu Thunderford, she might have been concerned about how close she was to the edge of the cliff and about the way the cloak caught the wind like a sail.

"It looks like they're heading towards the school entrance to the keep," Pasco reported, peering at the two men through the worsening weather. Tia tied the cloak around her neck, pulled the hood over her head and bent down to pick up her bag.

Pasco turned his gaze away from Llacheu Thunderford and his companion to see whether Tia was ready to continue. Only Tia wasn't there.

"*Tia!*" he yelled.

Chapter Seventeen

Magic Again

Tia was very confused. Pasco had shouted her name, then peered down the steep slope to the sea, shouted it again, put both hands up to the sides of his mouth to amplify his voice, then positively screamed her name. All the while, she had been standing there in the middle of the path, gawping at him. At first she thought it might be a bizarre joke, but that would not have been very Pasco-like. Besides, he looked genuinely distressed, as if he really thought she had tumbled down into the sea.

"I'm right here," she said, feeling a little confused.

"Aahhh!" Pasco leapt into the air and glanced all about him, looking absolutely terrified. "Tia? Where are you?"

She moved right in front of him, close enough that he could have reached out and touched her. "Can't you see me?"

Pasco removed his glasses, wiped them pointlessly on his raincoat and then replaced them. "N-n-no." He was panting and looked quite pale, but he seemed to be calming down.

"You mean the Mantle of Arthur really works?" Tia couldn't quite believe what she was about to ask. "Am I invisible?"

"Either that or you're playing some very unfunny joke on me." Pasco scowled at various patches of thin air in turn.

"But why has it suddenly started working now? Is it the rain? Does it need to be wet to work?"

"I don't know." Pasco's breathing was still shallow. "But can you take it off? You're freaking me out a bit."

It was very wet and windy by this point, and it felt wonderfully warm and dry beneath the ancient garment. But Pasco looked desperate, so Tia lowered the hood and began to undo the fastening around her neck.

"Aahhh!" Pasco leapt into the air again.

"What now?"

"Sorry. I just didn't realise you were so close!"

"You can see me now?" Tia was puzzled, as she still had the cloak over her shoulders. The magic of the mantle seemed to be sputtering on and off like an old car that was struggling to start.

"What did you do just now?" Pasco asked.

"What, just before you screamed?"

"I didn't scream," said Pasco with a pout. "It's quite a shock having someone disappear and reappear in front of you, you know!"

"I was just untying the cord to take the cloak off." Tia tied it back up under her chin. "And before that, I just took the hood off my head." She pulled the hood back over her head.

Pasco gasped. "You've vanished again!"

"It's the hood!" Tia momentarily lowered the hood, then covered her head again, a huge grin spreading across her face. She moved a few paces to the side and lowered the hood once more. In Pasco's eyes she had disappeared and then reappeared in another place, and Tia couldn't help but laugh aloud at his startled expression.

"Please stop doing that," he pleaded.

"Sorry, but this is pretty amazing!" Tia grinned.

"Yeah, I suppose it is." Pasco let out an exhausted sigh, as if he had been holding his breath. "Can we go now?"

"You're right, Pasco!" Tia's eyes lit up excitedly. "If I'm invisible I'll be able to get right up close to Llacheu Thunderford and find out what he's plotting."

She set off down the path towards the castle keep, jogging to catch up with the pair they had begun following.

"I meant go *home*," Pasco called after her as she

pulled the hood back over her head and vanished once more.

"You wait there," Tia's voice drifted back to him through the rain. "This'll be worth it, I promise!"

"All right," Pasco muttered sulkily, plonking himself down on the grass verge and pulling his hood down as far as it would go. "I'm finishing the chocolate raisins, though."

Tia soon caught sight of the two figures. They were huddled up against the wall of the castle keep, just next to the stone staircase that led up to the school entrance. Although there was no overhead cover, the angle of the driving rain meant that the great stone building gave them enough shelter to continue their conversation.

Although she was invisible, Tia crept up stealthily so as not to do anything that might alert them to her presence. She moved silently, trying not to disturb the bushes and grasses around her and keeping out of their eyeline in case the rain made curious shapes on her invisible form.

As she edged closer, Tia felt she recognised the second person after all. It appeared to be a middle-aged man, perhaps a little older than Llacheu Thunderford, his face more lined and worn. But he stood just as straight-backed and proud, a pair of thick, round glasses sitting on his large, hooked nose.

Once she had reached the wall of the keep and no longer felt the rain falling on her, she almost pulled back her hood without thinking, remembering just in time that this would break the spell of invisibility. She was close enough to hear the conversation and to get a good look at the second man.

What she saw prompted a gasp that would surely have been heard by the two men had it not been for the gusting wind and rain. The second man was Monsieur Moreau; the Frenchman who had caused the disturbance at the Tower of London just before Christmas.

His posture was completely different from that of the hunched old man who had hobbled over to speak to Uncle Ernie. He no longer had a moustache or wore a black cap, but he still had the same bushy eyebrows and crooked nose, and continued to clutch the battered brown leather bag. There was no doubt in Tia's mind that this was indeed the same person. As she listened, she realised he had no French accent either, which made her doubt that his name was Moreau at all.

"I'm sorry you've had so little help from our chaplain," Llacheu Thunderford drawled. "Locryn Meltwater can be a very stubborn man. He won't hear of my progressive ideas to keep Stormhaven going."

Tia nearly gasped again at the mention of her grandfather's name.

"Stubborn he may be," the other man replied in a decidedly English accent, "but no one else in this country is a greater authority on the looting of the abbeys during the Dissolution of the Monasteries. And it's a very particular piece of information I'm after. I don't think anyone else can help me." He paused and looked meaningfully at Llacheu over the top of his round glasses. "Unless there's someone else who might be able to grant me access to the records that will tell me what I want to know."

"You think those records are here?"

"Well, I've tried the National Archives at Kew and various regional archives without any success, and Reverend Meltwater does keep an extensive archive here."

"And here I was thinking you wanted me to try to charm Locryn into helping you," Llacheu smirked. "I was about to tell you I don't think I'd have the slightest chance. I'm not exactly in his inner circle of friends! But if it's access to Stormhaven's archives you desire, I think I may be able to help you." He pulled a large bunch of keys from his inside coat pocket. "I must warn you, though, that this may be a long search without Locryn's guidance. If you hadn't mentioned Her Ladyship you might have had more success with him. I'm afraid she's viewed with a certain amount of negativity by many older members of the Stormhaven community."

"You just get me to the right section and I'll be able to find what I'm after."

The two men climbed the staircase and Llacheu tried several keys in the lock before finding the right one. "This isn't the most direct route into the lower vaults of the library, but it'll get us out of this weather more quickly."

Tia dashed up the steps as quickly as she dared, but she wasn't quite quick enough. She barely heard the man she knew as Monsieur Moreau's last remark before the door was shut in her invisible face: "I'm most grateful to you, Mr Thunderford, and I'll be sure to recommend your plans for this place to Her Ladyship. She's always on the lookout for new investments; particularly those with historical interest."

Chapter Eighteen

Locryn Meltwater's Expertise

"I'm still confused." Pasco was trying to process everything Tia had relayed to him, but they were almost running along the path towards her grandpa's cottage as they spoke. It didn't help that Tia still had the hood of the cloak up to shield herself from the rain. Pasco soon discovered that it was very hard to concentrate on what someone was saying when you couldn't be entirely sure where their voice was coming from.

"So, this bloke reckons your grandpa knows some secret about the Coron Arthur?"

"It must be that." Tia lowered her hood, pushing on

the rusty gate that opened into the overgrown garden in front of Grandpa Locryn's tiny stone cottage as she rematerialised. "That's what Monsieur Moreau – or *Mr* Moreau… or whatever his real name might be – was looking for clues about at the Tower of London."

"But he didn't actually say anything about the crown?"

"Well, no, I guess not," Tia admitted as she knocked frantically at the door.

"You'd better put that away," Pasco said, eyeing the Mantle of Arthur, which was still draped over Tia's shoulders. "Wearing a cloak from the Dark Ages is bound to lead to a few awkward questions."

Tia just managed to stuff the cloak into her bag before Grandpa Locryn opened the door.

"Well, what a marvellous surprise!" The big, silver-bearded man hurriedly ushered them inside his home, then rounded on his granddaughter. "Tia, why aren't you wearing a coat?"

"I forgot it. Grandpa, I've got something really important to tell you." Tia didn't pause for breath until she had recounted all that she had overheard, though she carefully neglected to mention how she had managed to get close enough to hear it. Her grandfather made her say it all again, breathing properly between sentences, until he understood.

Grandpa Locryn frowned thoughtfully throughout Tia's monologue, his bushy white eyebrows meeting in the middle. But as soon as she finished, he simply shrugged and sighed. "Oh, well."

"Aren't you going to stop them?" pleaded Tia.

"Tia, dear, I don't *own* those records. I might have refused to help 'Mr Morris' – that's the name he gave me, at least – but Llacheu Thunderford has as much right to let someone into the archives as I do to decline a request. If they want to spend the rest of their evening ferreting through boxes, that's their business. I can't stop them."

"We could tell the police about this Mr Morris, though," suggested Pasco. "He'll be wanted for breaking into the archives at the Tower of London."

"Except he didn't break in, did he?" Grandpa Locryn was smiling, his tone patient. "He was wandering around where he shouldn't have been, and he would've got a telling off if the police had been able to catch him there and then. He might even have spent a night at the police station, but that's about it. The police certainly wouldn't be interested in him now."

"But he's going to get 'Her Ladyship' to invest in Llacheu Thunderford's scheme to build a Stormhaven hotel!"

"Llacheu can get whomever he wants to invest. He isn't going to get anywhere while Lord Reg is alive, and after he's gone, the rest of us on the board of trustees won't let anything happen to the school either."

Tia and Pasco glanced blankly at each other. Apparently, neither had any more arguments to put forward.

"Now, I'm going to call both your mothers, tell them that you've arrived on my doorstep dripping wet, and that you're staying for dinner. I'll walk the two of you home once you've dried out a bit."

Tia loved being at her grandpa's house. He had explained that it was previously a hut for goatherds who grazed their animals on the grassy slopes of the island before the village was built. They would sleep in the mezzanine loft, where Grandpa Locryn now slept, while the goats slept below. This ground floor area had been converted into an open-plan kitchen and living-room area. There was only one door apart from the front door, which led to a tiny bathroom. There was a wood burning stove in one corner of the open-plan area, with bookcases full of tatty old volumes covering every wall.

Tia, Pasco and Grandpa Locryn sat on wooden chairs that folded up and slid behind a cupboard when they weren't in use as they ate their bangers and mash on a table that folded down from the wall. Tia sometimes wondered whether, being such a tall and broad man, Grandpa Locryn ever felt cramped in his tiny house, but he always seemed very happy.

Tia was wearing an enormous dressing gown that Grandpa Locryn had given her to wear while her jumper and jeans dried out in front of the log burner.

She had finally calmed down and was resigned to the fact that Mr Morris was probably going to find out the information he was seeking and there was nothing they could do about it. "Why didn't you want to help Mr Morris?" Tia asked her grandpa as they ate.

"He mentioned he was acting on behalf of Lady Hilary Hendford. She's an infamous collector of historical artefacts and she doesn't mind bending the rules to get her hands on them. I said that I didn't think it was in the best interest of national heritage to help Her Ladyship."

"She wrote to Professor Hemyke's landlady saying she wanted to buy his old things!" Tia exclaimed. It seemed bizarre how many shadowy people she only knew a little about were connected to each other: Llacheu Thunderford, Mr Morris and now Lady Hendford, who she also suspected had some connection to the late Mr Silverman – the man who had tried to hijack their hunt for the Thirteen Treasures of Britain some months earlier, but had been trapped during the cave-in she and Pasco narrowly escaped.

"Did she?" Grandpa Locryn looked thoughtful for a moment, then shook his head as if he wasn't sure what to make of it. "She's involved in all sorts of dodgy dealings if the stories about her are to be believed."

"So…" Pasco swallowed his mouthful. Having been wearing a good rain jacket, he wasn't as wet as Tia, but Grandpa Locryn had lent him a pair of shorts so his sodden jeans could dry out. The shorts looked like extremely baggy trousers on Pasco. "Do you know what Mr Morris was looking for?"

Grandpa Locryn stroked his wiry beard, as if pondering whether or not to tell them what he knew. "He wanted to know about the accusations made against the last Abbot of Glastonbury Abbey. He wanted to know why Henry VIII's men killed him."

Grandpa Locryn picked up his knife and fork to resume his meal, but Tia was tantalised by the Glastonbury Abbey link.

"Why *did* they kill him?" she asked before he could get another forkful into his mouth.

Grandpa Locryn put down his cutlery and leaned back in his chair. "Have you heard of the Dissolution of the Monasteries?"

Pasco very tentatively said yes, as if he had heard of it but knew nothing more, while Tia simply shook her head blankly. Mr Morris's use of the term an hour earlier was the first time she had ever heard it.

"Well, during the sixteenth century Henry VIII made himself head of the new Church of England and began 'redistributing' the great wealth of the medieval monasteries. Hundreds of abbeys were demolished, some people were even killed and all the property belonging to the hundreds of monasteries across the country was seized."

"Why did he do that?" Tia asked.

"Oh, you could write a book on that!" her grandpa chuckled, adding flippantly: "In fact, I've written two myself!"

"Mr Morris said you were an expert on the looting of abbeys." Tia raised her eyebrows a little doubtfully as she spoke, hoping to goad her grandfather into sharing more. "In fact, he said you were *the* expert."

"Hard to believe, isn't it?" the old man chortled. He pushed his plate to one side, as if finally resigned to telling the children all they wanted to know. "The dissolution of the monasteries, like many other major historical events, was the result of powerful people – both inside and outside the Church – seeking their own best interests. And, like most major historical events, the people who came off worst were largely innocent. The Abbot of Glastonbury was most likely one such individual. King Henry's men did their best to accuse him of fiddling the abbey's accounts to line his own pockets, but they couldn't make anything stick. They didn't let him off, though. They executed him on top of Glastonbury Tor, the hilltop on the edge of the town."

"What were the details Mr Morris wanted to know?" Tia felt there was more; something that might be the final clue as to what had happened to the Coron Arthur when Glastonbury Abbey was seized by Henry VIII.

"One of the many historical treasures kept in the archive here at Stormhaven," Grandpa Locryn began, "is a report given by the men who dealt with the abbot on behalf of the king, and that's what he wanted to look at. I looked it up myself earlier today after Mr Morris had given up on me."

"And what did it say?" Tia asked as calmly as she could.

"It suggests that Henry's men wanted the abbot to reveal a secret, but they couldn't get it out of him. The report states that the abbot refused to speak of 'the secret of St Michael's Crypt'."

"St Michael's Crypt?" Tia puzzled aloud.

"A crypt is a kind of cellar beneath a church that's usually used to bury quite important people," her grandpa explained. "St Michael's is the church on top of Glastonbury Tor, the hilltop on the edge of the town where the abbot was executed, but no secret – or crypt – has ever been found beneath it, to my knowledge. It seems that either the abbot's executioners were misinformed about its existence or the abbot chose to take the secret to the grave with him." Grandpa Locryn stood up, as if to signal that there would be no more discussion. He smiled broadly before striding across to the refrigerator. "I think I've got some cheesecake we can finish off for pudding."

As her grandfather rummaged around in search of dessert, Tia whispered to Pasco, "I bet Mr Morris thinks Henry VIII's men were after the Coron Arthur. Once he's had a look at that report, he'll go looking for St Michael's Crypt."

Pasco nodded seriously.

"Ah, here it is!" Grandpa Locryn exclaimed.

As she tucked into her pudding, Tia's thoughts turned to Glastonbury and the possible secrets the town might be guarding.

I definitely need to get Mum and Dad to take me there for a look around, she thought to herself. She paused for a moment with the spoon halfway to her mouth. She wondered if that was the first time she had thought of her adoptive parents as 'Mum and Dad' without even a glimmer of it seeming strange to call them that.

Tia put the spoon in her mouth. The cheesecake tasted perfect.

Chapter Nineteen

The Sword in the Stone

As February gained momentum, the weather deteriorated into a succession of blustery gales blowing into Stormhaven from the Atlantic Ocean, broken only by days of drizzling rain whipped up by the swirling wind. Ten minutes outside was enough to leave those who ventured out looking as though they had been dunked in the sea.

The weather forced Mr Teague to rethink some of his outdoor activities. Their planned trip to an Iron Age hill fort was postponed, and after Tia and Rhea Bipul came close to being blown off the battlements one day, Mr Teague decided that they would stay indoors more than he had planned, at least for a few days. They got the foam weapons and armour out on a couple of occasions, pushing back the tables and benches in the feasting hall so they could delve a little deeper into medieval battle tactics. They also spent a lot of time in the library trying to find answers to questions that had arisen during the course of the term.

The class had hoped to get outside on the last day before the half-term break, but another gale had begun blowing branches, small seabirds and anything else it could get hold of across the lawn. The promise of worse to come meant Mr Teague had to come up with a new plan, and quickly. He bounded into the classroom after lunch looking very pleased with himself and announced that the class was in for a special treat. "Pack up your things, ready to go home. No, Gareth, it's not home time just yet – I have something even better than that planned!"

Gareth looked doubtful.

"We're going to spend the afternoon down at the blacksmith's with a couple of Stormhaven's experimental archaeologists, who are going to let us in on the mystical secrets of ancient metalworking!"

After a perilous journey across the windswept castle lawn, the warmth of the blacksmith's workshop with its blazing furnaces, smoky air and eerie glow did indeed feel quite mystical. The atmosphere was enhanced by the faint howling of a gale through the rafters overhead. Several members of the class gasped when Bran Corentyn's father and another member of the experimental archaeology team stepped out of a smoky corner wearing their leather blacksmith's aprons, awed by their almost magical entrance.

"Imagine for a moment," said Mr Corentyn, "that you live in the Stone Age. Everything you've ever seen or touched is made from some sort of natural material: wood, fur, earth or stone. You could hold any human-made object and be able to tell what it's made of just by looking and feeling. What would you make of a metal knife, though? Something that's as hard as rock but smooth and cool as water, and something that lasts longer than a hundred brittle flint blades."

He explained that metalworking had brought civilisation out of the Stone Age and into the Bronze Age. The discovery of what could be crafted using metal minerals rather than stone for tools, weapons and artwork had ushered in a whole new world of human accomplishment. Tia had heard the terms 'Stone Age' and 'Bronze Age' many times since moving to Stormhaven without them really meaning much to her. She felt as though they were beginning to make some sense.

As they demonstrated how metal was extracted from ore, which was mined from the earth, Mr Corentyn explained that the process had been seen as a supernatural one by most Bronze Age people, and that the role of the metalworker may have been considered to be somewhere between priest and craftsman. This view was held for thousands of years, especially by those from Viking cultures.

The class watched, entranced, as molten metal was poured into casts. Mr Corentyn extracted the cooled metal once it had set into various decorative shapes. Then the metalworkers polished some other pre-cast brooches to show how they would have been finished.

As they poured the last of the molten metal into a large stone cast, Mr Teague drew alongside Tia, who was standing with Pasco, Meghan and Bran. "Some historians think this may be the origin of the 'Sword in the Stone' legend," he whispered as Mr Corentyn separated the two halves of the stone cast. It was rough and unfinished, but the woman assisting Bran's dad pulled out an object that was unmistakably a sword blade. The molten metal had seeped between the two stone halves a little, giving the weapon a jagged edge that caught the glow of the furnace, appearing to burn as if in homage to the flames that had given it life. "It's been suggested that this Bronze Age method of forging a sword may have carried over into the Iron Age as a ceremonial act during the coronation of a new warlord or chieftain. In which case, a historical Arthur figure may well have 'pulled' a sword from a stone cast during his rise to power."

"So that's how Excalibur was made!" said Meghan in an awed voice.

"Actually," Pasco said absent-mindedly, still watching as the sword was given a handle wrapped in leather straps, "the Sword in the Stone and Excalibur were different swords in the legends."

Mr Teague and the three other children turned to face Pasco, who didn't seem to notice. He continued to talk casually without shifting his gaze from the demonstration: "Merlin got Excalibur from the Lady in the Lake and gave it to Arthur after the sword he pulled from the stone broke in a battle. I guess if the Sword in the Stone were a Bronze Age sword it would have broken in a battle if it were used against Iron Age swords."

"Very impressive, Pasco," beamed Mr Teague.

Pasco reddened, realising their focus was fixed on him.

"Speaking of which, I think Mr Corentyn's moving on to Iron Age metalwork now," Mr Teague said to deflect attention away from Pasco.

Bran's father did go on to talk about the discovery of methods for working harder metals, which was what marked the Iron Age. Although Bronze Age techniques were still used to create ornamental items for decorative or ceremonial uses, people began using other metals for tools and weapons that were too strong to be fully melted. Rather than pouring molten metal, these items were made by heating the tougher metals to soften them, then hammering them into shape.

Mr Corentyn demonstrated these new techniques by hammering a piece of metal into a spearhead. He pulled the glowing metal from the furnace and hammered it until it cooled to a darker colour. Then he plunged it back into the burning coals again and repeated the process.

"But it would have been a bit silly for Arthur to use a weaker sword in a battle against swords he knew would be stronger, wouldn't it?" Tia whispered to Mr Teague.

"Yes," her bearded teacher acknowledged. "But in the same way that the story of Arthur pulling a sword from a stone might be a case of legend shadowing a historical fact, the story of his sword breaking and being replaced by something stronger may be a shadow of the fact that Bronze Age weapons weren't as tough as those of the Iron Age."

He smiled warmly and leaned in closer so that no one else would be able to hear. "We know from experience, don't we, Tia, that there are often remarkable truths at the heart of our myths and legends?" He winked, then turned his attention back to Mr Corentyn.

Tia gazed curiously at her teacher for a while. She knew he was very close to her parents and wondered whether he knew about her adventure in the Chamber of the Thirteen Treasures. She had told him of her connection to the legend of the Thirteen Treasures herself, and recalled how Mr Teague had convinced her that she would find truth in her exploration of the mysteries, regardless of whether she discovered any actual facts. And he had been right. She was no closer to being able to narrate her birth story or name her birth parents, but she did know herself better.

Tia sighed. Truth might be the most important thing, but facts were easier to get her head round and it would be nice to get her hands on a few of them every so often.

The demonstration ended with each member of the class being given the chance to don a pair of safety glasses and fireproof gloves, and then to pour a tiny amount of molten metal into the cast of a small brooch to take home with them. Clutching their cooled but still warm creations tightly in their fists, the children stepped out into the elements to brave the journey home, with Mr Teague waving and trying his best to wish them a fun-filled half-term week over the roar of the wind.

As thoughts of St Michael's Crypt and the Coron Arthur continued to buzz around her head during the half-term break, it wasn't long before Tia asked her mother if they could take a trip to Glastonbury soon.

Mrs Trevelyan gazed at her daughter thoughtfully for a while before answering. "You know," she said with a smile, "I thought you'd ask that on the way home from London. What are you hoping to find there?"

Tia was drying the dishes while her mother washed. "I know there hasn't been much at the abbey since the Dissolution." She paused for effect after dropping in the term that had meant nothing to her until recently, and Mrs Trevelyan looked obligingly impressed at her daughter's use of the word. "But I'd still like to see it. I know it's a bit silly that I keep latching on to anything at all to do with Arthur, but it feels like I'll understand myself better if I find out all I can about him… the history *and* the legend. I know that doesn't really make sense."

"It makes just as much sense as people who 'find themselves' while climbing a mountain, trekking across a desert or doing some other adventurous thing." Mrs Trevelyan handed Tia another plate to dry. "Your dad and I are delighted that your adventure involves so much history," she added with a smile.

Tia grinned back. She felt quietly confident that she would get her trip to Glastonbury. "I'd like to go up the Tor, too," she added casually.

"Sounds like you've got it all planned out." Mrs Trevelyan dropped the last of the cutlery into the drying rack and dried her hands on a tea towel. "But I don't think we'll be able to manage it this week, I'm afraid. Dad and I are quite busy. How about we go for a day trip in a couple of weeks?"

Tia said that would be great and placed the last fork in the drawer before turning to leave the kitchen.

"Tia," her mother said, fixing her daughter with an anxious gaze as she turned back round. "Do you think you're going to find the Coron Arthur or something?"

Tia knew she couldn't lie to her mother, but she managed a scoff and pulled a face that she hoped said, "What a ridiculous idea that would be!". Then she left the room as quickly as possible in case her mother asked any more probing questions.

Chapter Twenty

Camelot and the Round Table

A couple of days later, as the Trevelyans were just finishing dinner, there was a knock at the door.

"I'll get it!" Meghan leapt out of her seat and sprinted down the corridor. "Mr Teague!" she exclaimed on opening the door.

"Hi, Meghan," they heard a breathless voice say at the door. "Can I come in for a bit? I've got some news for you all."

Mr and Mrs Trevelyan's heads snapped up on hearing this, and Tia saw them grin broadly at each other before rising to their feet.

"It's Mr Teague!" Meghan announced as she re-entered the room, followed by their teacher.

Tia was suddenly aware that she was the only person who was sitting down. For some reason, the attitude of the adults made her feel as though she should also be standing, although no one made any motion to her to do so, as they were all too busy beaming expectantly at each other. Meghan was glancing from one face to another, wide-eyed, clearly expecting something very exciting to happen. Tia just felt confused, which in turn made her feel on edge.

"I just asked Iris to marry me!" Mr Teague blurted out with a slightly crazed expression on his face. "I'd like you to be my best man, Tom," he added, turning to Mr Trevelyan.

"Hold on," Mr Trevelyan said, looking very serious. "You haven't told us whether she said yes yet."

"Oh, Tom!" Mrs Trevelyan gave her husband a playful punch on the shoulder. "Of course she said yes. Congratulations, Callum!" Mrs Trevelyan crossed the room, kissed Mr Teague on the cheek and then hugged him warmly.

"Congratulations, mate!" laughed Mr Trevelyan, wrapping his wife and his friend up in his arms.

Meghan had been bouncing up and down since Mr Teague made the announcement and could contain her excitement no longer. With a loud squeak she joined the group hug, flinging herself at the embracing adults.

Once again, Tia felt like the odd one out. As she shuffled over to the others, her father reached out an arm and pulled her in.

The rest of the meal was forgotten. Mr and Mrs Trevelyan grabbed some glasses, a bottle of lemonade and a bottle of another fizzy drink for the adults, and they all bundled into the sitting room to celebrate.

Tia tried to relax in an armchair. She continued to gaze at the adults, who didn't stop smiling the whole evening. She also looked at her delighted sister, wishing she was able to throw herself into everything in such a wholehearted and carefree manner without the unknown causing such tension within her. It wasn't too long before she was able to give herself up to the joy of the evening.

Mr Trevelyan got a fire going and they spent the rest of the evening drinking and discussing wedding plans. Mr Teague said they wanted to have a simple wedding in Miss Williams' home village in Somerset. Her parents were farmers and owned a meadow near the village church, where they could put up a marquee.

"Any guests who want to stay could camp in the field," he said. "Cheap accommodation might be a bit tricky to find locally, though it's not far from Bristol."

"Sounds like a lot of it's already sorted," said Mr Trevelyan, sticking another log on the fire.

"There'll be a lot of other things to sort out," Mrs Trevelyan pointed out to her husband. "Tell Iris I'll help with whatever I can, Callum."

"Thanks. She's going to try to book the church tomorrow, but we want Locryn to marry us. I'll ask him as soon as we know about the church, but all being well we'd like to set a date for the end of July." Mr Teague took a contented sip of his drink. "Then we're planning to hire a campervan and travel around Europe over the summer holidays."

The mood grew sleepy as the fire died down to embers, but no one seemed in any rush to end the evening. Meghan sat in the corner of the room with her father, advising him on his best man's speech. At first Mr Trevelyan listened with an amused grin, but his face soon changed to an expression of concentration. He evidently felt Meghan had some genuinely good ideas.

Tia had moved out of the armchair and was sprawled out on a rug, leaning against the sofa where her mother and Mr Teague were discussing which friends and family he hoped would travel from far and wide for the wedding. She was beginning to contentedly slip off to sleep when she became aware that Mr Teague was talking to her. She turned her head so she could see both adults on the sofa.

"Did you enjoy that trip on Friday, Tia?" Mr Teague asked.

"Yeah," Tia yawned. "I think I get the whole Bronze Age–Iron Age thing now. And I liked what you said about the Sword in the Stone."

"We talked a bit about the shadowy connections

between legends and the way things really were in the past," Mr Teague explained to Mrs Trevelyan. "I think Tia's becoming quite an Arthur enthusiast!"

"Yes, I've noticed." She smiled warmly at her daughter.

"Speaking of which," the teacher sighed, "it's a shame we had to postpone the Cadbury Castle trip."

An image of a palace made out of chocolate jumped into Tia's mind, but Mr Teague quickly explained that it was an Iron Age hill fort in Somerset that many archaeologists believed may have given rise to the legend of Camelot.

"There's no direct link to anyone named Arthur," he said, "but there is no other site in Britain that saw such extensive use – both domestic and military – during the brief period after the Romans left and before the west of England became truly Anglo-Saxon."

"Can we still go soon, though?" Tia asked eagerly, her interest piqued, as ever, by the mention of an Arthurian connection.

"We'll see," conceded Mr Teague. "I do have a lot of other exciting stuff planned, you know, so it might have to wait a while. I should warn you, though, that there's not much to see there apart from mounds of earth. Like all other forts of its time, Cadbury Castle was made of wood, so it's all rotted away."

"All the same, I'd still love to go some time," Tia said keenly.

The evening finished with Meghan energetically telling Mr Teague about their planned trip to Bala Lake in the summer and all the adventure sports they were hoping to try out, as well as the underwater archaeology they were going to help with. Mr Teague assured her that the wedding would take place early enough in the summer holidays that it wouldn't impact on their plans, and then the girls were finally ushered upstairs to bed.

One stormy afternoon during the first week back at school, Tia was in the library waiting for her father. He had arranged to meet her there when he had finished work, as Mrs Trevelyan was taking Meghan to the dentist. Tia was sitting with Pasco, who spent most after-school sessions in the library where his mother worked.

Tia was reading a book about Arthurian legends, a subject she always seemed to return to nowadays whenever she wanted to read a story. She sometimes read other myths and legends from ancient Britain, but usually with the slim hope of finding some new insight into her quest for the Hallows of Arthur.

Pasco was reading a book about hill forts. The two friends had begun reading up on this topic after Tia told Pasco what Mr Teague had said about Cadbury Castle possibly being Camelot. For Pasco, this had led on to wider reading about hill forts, while Tia had gone back to myths and legends once she had found out all she could about Cadbury Castle.

She was reading the story of how Morgan le Fey stole the scabbard of Excalibur from King Arthur because the scabbard protected whoever wore it during a battle. She stopped when she heard Pasco gasp, and looked up to see him darting off down one of the aisles, leaving the book he had been reading lying open on the floor in front of his favourite bean bag. Tia peered at the open pages, spotting an illustration of a group of warriors standing around in a circle.

Pasco soon returned, clutching another book. He plonked himself down on the bean bag and began riffling through the pages, clearly looking for something specific.

Tia was about to return to her book when Pasco exclaimed, "Aha!" He laid the book down next to the first, slapped the open page triumphantly and looked over at Tia with a broad grin on his face.

"Found something interesting?" she enquired with a raised eyebrow.

"Well, I was reading this a while ago," he said, holding up the book he had just fetched, "when I was trying to research stuff that once belonged to Arthur. It said the Round Table legend might have come from the way warlords held their gatherings in circles. It got me thinking that Arthur's Round Table might have been a place; not a table at all."

Tia nodded to show that she was following, and as Pasco paused for breath she considered what Mr Teague had said about legends being shadows of historical fact. She also thought about what Pasco had said months earlier concerning his dad's comment that legends may be born from half-forgotten memory or half-understood experience, but are never made up out of thin air.

"I've just read in this one," Pasco continued, pointing to the first book he had been reading, "that warlords probably met in circles like this to make agreements between different hill forts or to form battle plans. And look what they're meeting *around*!"

Tia peered at the picture of the circular gathering of chieftains on the page that lay open on the floor before them. At the centre of the circle of warriors was a small, round object, flat to the ground. "A tiny round table?" she asked tentatively.

"Exactly! Only it's not actually a table. This book says: 'It is thought that the leading chieftain may have laid down his *shield*. Everyone would have gathered around that.'"

Pasco continued to grin broadly at her until Tia fully caught up. "So Arthur's Round Table was actually his shield!" she concluded.

"I reckon so. It makes a whole lot more sense for the real-life Arthur than a huge round wooden table, doesn't it?"

Tia was instantly convinced. The line "Where Arthur

held court, his men around him" indicated that Arthur's shield was one of the hallows. The shadow of this historical fact had shown itself in the legend of King Arthur's Round Table.

For a moment Tia felt jubilant, but she was quickly brought down to earth when she realised this meant that they would actually need to find Arthur's shield at some point.

And she didn't have a clue how to go about it.

Chapter Twenty-One

Fear Returns

Looking back, Tia was able to recall the tiniest details from the moments just before her parents gave her their harrowing news. She remembered the daffodils she had seen walking home from school with Meghan and the anticipation of spring they had kindled in her. She remembered how clean the houses had looked after a day of being washed by the finest early March drizzle, and she remembered glancing down at her shoes as she brushed them on the doormat and thinking how scuffed they looked.

But the world outside was forgotten as she and her sister noticed their parents, poised and waiting for them, in the living room. They instantly knew that something was wrong. Not only were their parents never both home at this time of day, but they also never looked so downcast and ashen-faced.

Their mother was standing before the fireplace with red eyes that had only just stopped crying. Their father was sitting in an armchair beside the window with his head in his hands.

Mrs Trevelyan looked at the girls and beckoned them into the room, but Tia wasn't sure that their father had registered their presence. She felt an instinct taking over, as if someone were hollowing her feelings out from her core to protect her from the pain her parents' words were about to unleash. *If you want to stay safe*, a voice seemed to be whispering to her, *you'll need to switch your feelings off.*

Tia felt numb. She had no recollection of entering the room, but she somehow found herself sitting on the sofa next to Meghan. Her mother was talking to them from what seemed like miles away over on the other side of the room.

"We've had a message from Nana Ollie," she said. "She's not very well… not very well at all." She swallowed before continuing. "She went into hospital a couple of days ago, having passed out on a dive boat while cleaning her scuba gear. They've done a lot of tests, and…" Her voice faltered for a moment. "It looks like she has cancer."

Silent tears fell from her mother's eyes as she spoke,

and Tia could feel Meghan trembling next to her. Her father looked up for the first time and she saw that he too was crying. Tia's protective internal instinct was to keep them all at arm's length, yet a part of her longed to share her family's sadness.

Surely this was something it was right to be sad about.

"Is she going to die?" Meghan asked. Her voice cracked as she spoke.

Tia heard her sister begin to sob, but did not turn to look at her. She continued to stare blankly ahead, her body rigid.

"No one's told her that," Mrs Trevelyan said softly, dropping to her knees in front of her daughters and taking Meghan's hand. "But the cancer's already quite advanced, and she has a big fight on her hands."

"She's a good fighter, though!" Meghan sobbed defiantly.

Mrs Trevelyan nodded and put her arms around her crying daughter.

Tia felt as though she wasn't really present. She didn't know how she was supposed to feel, and was only faintly aware of her father moving across the room to sit beside her and put an arm around her shoulders.

But she heard the words he whispered into her ear: "Whatever it is you're feeling right now, Tia, it's okay to feel it."

His words seemed to echo around the empty hollow inside her. She couldn't say exactly what she was feeling, but she gradually stopped panicking about trying to pin the feeling down. She dwelt on her father's words as she thought about her grandmother and how much she loved her. She thought of the faithfulness Nana Ollie had shown in taking them up to Kirkburn in November. Without her help, Tia would not be following her current path.

The four of them consoled one another in silence for several minutes, and the rest of the evening was punctuated with long periods of quiet as they each became lost in their own thoughts at various points. But there was also plenty of talk as the girls asked questions and the adults shared more details.

"Nana Ollie will need to have a few more tests," Mr Trevelyan told them over dinner, "and she'll need a lot of rest after that. But she's hoping to finish everything up in the Caribbean in the next month or two and then move back to the UK for treatment."

"She's coming to Stormhaven!" Meghan exclaimed, desperately trying to cling to something positive.

"She'd love to be here," Mr Trevelyan said hesitantly, "but it'll be best if she's living somewhere near a hospital for her treatment."

"It *would* be good for her to be near the sea, though," Tia said, poking at her dinner with her fork.

There was a thoughtful pause before Mrs Trevelyan continued. "She won't be far away, and we're definitely going to see a lot of her. We'll make sure she gets to the sea as much as possible."

When they eventually made their way up to bed, Meghan used the journey upstairs as a transition into a different thought world. Seeing the map of the island Pasco had given Tia lying on the desk in their room, she asked if they could do some exploring in the morning in an attempt to find more of the features marked on the ancient chart.

Tia agreed. She had no desire to spend time with anyone outside the family, and she liked the idea of being out and about with her sister, trying not to think about anything much at all.

She sat on the edge of her bed for some time, replaying the events of the evening and everything her parents had said about Nana Ollie. She was terrified of losing her grandmother.

Tia had known fear her whole life as a quiet backdrop to her day-to-day experience, yet this was different somehow. For once, she was not *scared* of feeling scared. This fear wasn't making her feel alone; in fact, it was driving her closer to those around her, who shared her fears.

After a while she found that – despite her fears – she was able to lie down. She was able to shut her eyes and, very quickly, slipped into an exhausted sleep.

Chapter Twenty-Two

Looking for a Distraction

When Tia opened her eyes in the morning, she thought she could see Meghan staring at her from across the room, perched on the edge of her bed. She was already dressed, her hair held back with an indigo bandana, a packed rucksack leaning against the bed beside her feet.

This wouldn't have been the first time Tia had woken to find her sister staring at her, waiting for her to wake. But this time Meghan was actually staring into thin air, lost in her thoughts and completely unaware that Tia had awoken. She didn't need to ask what Meghan was thinking about.

After a while, Tia yawned and stretched, and Meghan smiled wearily at her, explaining that she had already been up for an hour and had packed everything they would need as they explored the island.

Once she was dressed, Tia debated whether to pack Arthur's cloak again, given how useful it had been while she and Pasco were following the map a couple of weeks ago. But she still hadn't told Meghan that the mantle really did make its wearer invisible, and she felt too emotionally exhausted to talk about it now. What she really needed was a morning of wandering over the island, allowing Meghan to take the lead and soaking in the peaceful atmosphere of Stormhaven.

It seemed this was also what Meghan needed. She was much quieter than usual as they picked their way across the island, but she was happy to be out, and it cheered Tia to see her sister looking so upbeat.

Their exploration went much the same way as Tia and Pasco's had. The landmarks on the ancient map, such as the standing stones, were easy enough to find, but it seemed as though every one of the footpaths crisscrossing the island on the chart had been swallowed up by centuries of bracken and brambles. The difference was that Meghan was thrilled to find herself hacking her way through the undergrowth and soon began talking about clearing every path on the island.

"It would be brilliant, wouldn't it," Meghan called to Tia over her shoulder as they made their way towards their third standing stone of the morning, "to remake all the ancient pathways?"

Meghan had found a strong stick, which she swung from side to side to clear the foliage blocking their path. Tia got the impression her sister was imagining herself as an intrepid adventurer making her way through unexplored Amazonian rainforest.

"It's a bit weird, though, isn't it?" Meghan continued between swipes of her imaginary machete. "I mean, you'd think at least some of the old paths would still exist. People have lived on the island for hundreds of years and there are paths between all the standing stones nowadays. It's as if, at some point between when that map was drawn and now, someone just decided they wanted a whole new set of paths, planted loads of ferns along the old ones, and cut completely new ones through the bushes."

Tia was too busy trying to dodge the branches whipping back at her after Meghan had pushed them to one side to give her sister's words much thought at first. As they finally hacked their way out of the undergrowth, she began to wonder whether Meghan had a point, but she suddenly became distracted by the memory of an event that had taken place during her first twenty-four hours in Stormhaven.

They had emerged into a small clearing surrounded by thorn bushes. At the centre was a crater roped off with black-and-yellow hazard tape. Tia knew the crater opened into an underground cavern where a once-standing stone lay. The stone had fallen from the ground above it after Tia had laid a hand on what she thought was a symbol like the one on her pendant: a Solomon's knot.

Was that really only six months ago?

"Remember when you pushed that stone over?" Meghan laughed. "It's a shame they couldn't lift it back out, but I guess there are seven more. And it was a brilliant adventure!"

Tia rubbed the engraved cross symbol on her pendant and stared into the hole, not wanting to look at her sister. The way Meghan had accused her of pushing the ancient stone over always bugged her. Perhaps it was due to some lingering embarrassment that made her not want to talk about the whole episode any more than she had to, but for some reason Tia had never really told Meghan about the engraving she thought she had seen on the stone.

"I didn't push it over, you know," Tia said, still gazing into the crater. "I thought it had my pendant symbol engraved on it." She held it up. "So I put my hand over it and it just moved."

"Like in the church in Kirkburn?" Meghan asked in an awed whisper, gazing wide-eyed into the crater as if she might see the tiny engraving on the stone if she stared into the gloom for long enough.

"Kind of," Tia conceded.

The font that bore the Solomon's knot in Kirkburn had glided back relatively smoothly to reveal a secret passageway leading to the Thirteen Treasures of Britain, whereas this standing stone had simply toppled over and crashed into the underground cavern, as if the magic had a glitch in it. But it occurred to Tia that both cases involved the engraved stone moving at her touch.

"Have you tried looking for that symbol on any of the other standing stones?" Meghan asked.

"No," Tia replied. "I don't want any more standing stones collapsing on me!"

Meghan looked disappointed for a moment, then her whole face lit up as if she had just thought of something wonderful. "What if this is actually an entrance to another magical treasure chamber?" she said, beginning to bounce excitedly. "Another of the Hallows of Arthur might be down there!"

"We were down there, remember?" Tia said doubtfully. "It was just a load of smugglers' boxes and barrels."

"We didn't explore along the cavern, though, did we?" Meghan's eyes were growing even wider as she peered into the crater. "Remember? The passage went off in that direction… and in that direction." Meghan pointed first one way and then back along the roughly hacked path they had just cleared and struggled along as they followed the map to reach the stone.

Tia gazed thoughtfully into the hole. Perhaps her sister had a point. There surely couldn't be too many ancient stones lying around that would respond magically to her touch, and the only other time it happened she had wound up finding the Mantle of Arthur.

"Tia," Meghan said in a quietly serious voice.

Tia was startled by the change in her sister's tone and looked up to see her holding the copy of the old chart they had been following. Meghan was glancing from the map to the crater, and then back at the map again.

"The path we just followed to get here," Meghan continued thoughtfully, "runs precisely above the underground passageway. And look, the map shows another path ending exactly where Merlin's Cave is in the bay." She looked up at Tia with a startled expression on her face. "What if this map doesn't show ancient paths *across* the island, but ancient paths *through* the island? What if it's a map of the caverns?"

Tia couldn't help scoffing at the idea at first, but she quickly began to wonder whether Meghan might be on to something. She looked intently at the map when Meghan passed it to her. *Is that why none of the paths marked on the chart match up with an existing pathway on the island?*

When Tia glanced back at her sister, she saw that Meghan was rummaging through her rucksack for something. Tia was about to say that she thought Meghan may be right, but was disconcerted to see her sister pull a bundle of rope out of her bag.

"You brought climbing rope with you? What's that for?" Tia asked, already knowing the answer.

"I'm going to check if the other passage follows the direction of the path on the map," Meghan answered distractedly as she searched around for something strong to tie the end of the rope to.

"That black-and-yellow tape is there for a reason, you know."

"Yeah," said Meghan as she passed the rope around the thick trunk of a bush and tied it off with several half-hitches. "It's there so nobody falls down the hole without seeing it. I'm going down on purpose."

"It's there because it's *dangerous*!" said Tia in an exasperated voice.

"It's not dangerous!" Meghan said dismissively, taking a compass out of her bag. "We've been down there ourselves. It's fine!"

"You sprained your ankle last time we went down there," Tia reminded her.

"Which is why I'll be using a rope this time," said Meghan, as if Tia were fussing unnecessarily.

Tia didn't quite know how to reason with her sister, and was still opening and shutting her mouth in the hope that some fresh argument would come to her, when Meghan ducked under the tape, threw the other end of the rope into the hole and readied herself to abscil down it.

"Don't worry," Meghan said calmly. "I just want to check which direction the passage goes off in. I'm not going far into it; I forgot to bring a torch."

"Forgot?! Why would anyone even think of bringing a torch on a morning walk?"

But she was talking to herself. Meghan had already descended into the crater with the map and compass bulging out of her pocket. For a minute or two Tia listened in silence to the sound of Meghan scrabbling against the earthen walls and breathing heavily. Then there was a solid-sounding thud and Meghan called up to confirm that she had arrived at the bottom without spraining anything.

"Yep, both passages definitely follow the path marked on the map," she said after a pause, during which Tia assumed she was checking the direction of the caverns using the compass. "But we can't really be sure until we've actually followed one of them for a while. I wish I'd brought my torch!"

Tia was glad she hadn't because it meant her sister would soon be making her way back up out of the pit, but she couldn't really relax until Meghan had untied the rope and started coiling it up again.

"Maybe if we just nip home and grab a couple of torches…" Meghan began.

Tia stopped her. "Look at this," she said holding the map up. She knew her sister was bound to suggest they return to the crater properly equipped for going further down the passages, so she had been scouring the map, trying to come up with a way of exploring the cave network that didn't involve any abseiling. "Just here, by this other standing stone," Tia continued, pointing to a mark denoting the stone that stood in the middle of the island. "It looks like a path starts just here. If this really is a map of the caverns, that must be a cave that serves as an entrance. Maybe we could get in that way?"

"Great idea, sis! I don't know any caves other than Merlin's Cave, but that's probably just because it's covered with bushes and has been forgotten about."

It was approaching lunchtime, so they set off for home, with Meghan talking excitedly about setting off again with torches in the afternoon.

However, Meghan's plans were scuppered when the heavens suddenly opened after lunch. The rain lasted for the rest of the weekend and Meghan spent the time skulking around like a caged animal, glancing alternately from her compass to the window in the hope that it would eventually stop.

Tia, on the other hand, was glad for the excuse to postpone their expedition. It had been a good distraction, and she did want to find out whether the map depicted Stormhaven's cave network, but she simply didn't have the energy. Her thoughts flitted from the Hallows of Arthur to the hollows of Stormhaven, and she wondered whether there really could be another artefact of Arthur's hidden away within the island's caverns and tunnels. *There has to be some reason for the standing stone to be engraved with a Solomon's knot.*

But her thoughts were never very far from Nana

Ollie. She wondered what her grandmother was doing at various points in the day, and how she would be feeling. Tia longed to tell Nana Ollie, as her father had told her, that whatever she might be feeling, it was okay to feel it.

Chapter Twenty-Three

Under the Island

Tia knew that, come the first dry weekend, Meghan would insist that they begin their exploration of the caverns. Sure enough, Tia found herself hiking back up the hill with her sister the following Saturday less than an hour after sunrise, their rucksacks packed with more equipment and provisions than they could ever possibly need. Meghan had prepared for the worst and made sure they brought all they would need if they found themselves trapped in a cave or if one of them broke a leg.

It was this sort of talk that had resulted in Pasco declining their offer to join them, a decision Meghan simply couldn't understand. "Your loss, but at least we won't have to tell anyone what we're doing now," she had said with a shrug when he said no. "I was thinking we might have to tell Mum and Dad, just in case something happened. They might have stopped us going in the first place, but now we don't need to tell them because you can always let them know if we don't make it back."

Mrs Trevelyan was always a little inclined to worry, but this was usually balanced by her husband's carefree enthusiasm. However, Mr Trevelyan had been very subdued this past week. He usually announced his arrival home in the evening with a loud greeting to the whole family as soon as he stepped through the door, then gave a detailed account over dinner – whether anyone had asked for it or not – of any long-lost historical secrets he had discovered that day.

This last week he had slipped into the house quite noiselessly, offering few details about his work as they ate. Tia knew without asking that it was his mother, Nana Ollie, who was occupying his thoughts.

Meghan hadn't quite been her usual self, either. Talk of exploring Stormhaven's caverns was the only thing that had produced any spark of the enthusiasm and energy with which she typically embraced every aspect of life. It was as if the thought of the expedition was a form of therapy for her, and this was at least part of the reason why Tia had indulged her sister's planning conversations over the last week.

As they made their way up the hill towards the standing stone that seemed to mark the entrance to the cave, Tia felt a mixture of anxiety and excitement growing within her. She still had trouble distinguishing between these two feelings, but was at least learning to recognise the conflict of emotions that so often churned in her stomach.

The stone sprang into view as they rounded a particularly large gorse bush. It was slightly taller than Meghan, and the sisters would have just about been able to link arms around it. Its rough edges had been smoothed by centuries of salty sea storms and was covered in patches of lichen.

The pair stared at it for a while before Meghan spoke. "Why don't you check it for your Solomon's knot symbol?" she said in an excited whisper. "I'll look for the cave entrance."

Meghan darted away and began delving enthusiastically into the bushes behind the stone, but Tia stood motionless for a while. She wasn't sure whether she wanted to find anything carved into the stone or not. She couldn't explain why, but she had a feeling that this was not the way to go about finding the Hallows of Arthur.

After a minute or two, she reluctantly stepped forward and placed her hand on the surface of the ancient rock. Closing her eyes to shut out the world around her, she felt an almost indiscernible tremble through her fingertips. The sensation passed silently up her arm, making the fine hairs from her wrist to her neck stand on end.

As she opened her eyes, she found herself almost involuntarily searching the marks on the stone for any sort of carving, a sense of dread rising within her as her hands and eyes probed the surface.

"Tia!"

It was as though Meghan's voice had jolted her out of a dream. She recoiled from the rock with a gasp.

"Can you give me a hand with this bush?"

Tia edged warily around the stone, as if worried it might lash out at her. She almost tripped over Meghan as she backed away in the direction of her sister's voice.

"Watch out! The thorns on this bramble are huge." Wearing a pair of tough rigging gloves, Meghan was holding back the branches of a large bush to expose its trunk. "Look in my bag," she instructed Tia. "There's another pair of gloves and Grandpa Locryn's garden loppers in there. I think we need to get rid of this bush. There's definitely something behind all this." She nodded towards the mass of foliage behind the bush she was wrestling with.

As Tia rummaged through the rucksack – sifting past a climbing rope, torches, snacks, everything they might need to start a small campfire and even a crowbar – she marvelled at the amount of preparation Meghan had put into this trip.

Once Tia had donned the gloves and strained to cut through the woody stem of the plant, Meghan rolled it to one side, then immediately moved forward to begin clearing out the thickets behind it. "Pass me the loppers," she said in a voice filled with glee.

Tia handed the tool to her sister, then glanced back over her shoulder at the ancient rock behind her. She almost felt as though it were watching her, even calling to her. For a moment she considered returning to it, but then she forced her head back round to gauge her sister's progress in an attempt to block out the stone's voice.

Meghan was merrily making her way through the gorse and bramble bushes. She had cut a small tunnel through the foliage using the borrowed loppers. Only her feet were visible as she continued to chop away, stopping occasionally to throw a branch out behind her. "I can definitely see something back here," she cried, panting with excitement and exertion. "It looks like it might be an opening!"

As her sister delved deeper into the bushes, her feet disappearing completely from view, Tia felt a mounting urge to turn back towards the stone once more. All at once, there came the sound of wood snapping and a great amount of earth moving and stones scraping against one another, instantly followed by a shriek of surprise from Meghan.

"Meghan!" Tia shouted, falling to her knees. She scrabbled into the gap her sister had made through the undergrowth, paying no attention to the brambles as they scratched at her hands and face. She couldn't believe this was happening again. She hadn't even touched a Solomon's knot symbol this time!

"I'm OK!"

Tia was relieved to hear her sister's voice sounding clear and not too far away.

"I think I've found the tunnel entrance," Meghan continued, "but I can't really see anything. Can you grab my bag and pass me a torch?"

Tia backed out of the bushes, snatched up the rucksack and dived back in, fumbling for a torch as she went. Once she had pulled one out and turned it on, she was able to see a hollow in the earth leading down between two large boulders, completely hidden by the undergrowth. She crawled further forward and directed the torchlight down into the hole, only to see her sister gazing back up at her.

Meghan hadn't fallen far at all, and Tia was able to pass her the torch without needing to fully stretch out her arm. She looked filthy – apparently most of the earth had fallen on top of her as she fell – but seemed unharmed. Her grubby face looked positively thrilled at having fallen into a secret tunnel that had been hidden and forgotten about for centuries.

"Pass me the bag, and then you come down this slope, too," said Meghan. "It's not that steep and it feels quite solid, so we'll be able to get back up easily enough."

Once Tia had joined her sister and switched on the second torch, she was able to take in their surroundings. They were standing in a narrow passageway that an adult would have had to stoop to pass through, but in which they could just about stand upright without hitting their heads on the stony ceiling. The walls were solid rock that narrowed together at their feet, so that there wasn't really any flat floor, but rather a sort of stony valley with pointed rocks they would have to negotiate if they wanted to proceed.

Meghan didn't stop to think twice about whether they should go further into the tunnel but she at least checked briefly that Tia was ready before setting off with a torch in one hand and the map, stowed away in a protective plastic sleeve, in the other. It wasn't long before she had to fold the map away in her pocket because both girls needed to hold on to the wall of the passageway to steady themselves as they picked their way along the uneven passageway.

Judging by how rocky and uneven all the surfaces were, the tunnel looked as though it was natural rather than man-made, although they could tell from a rusty old candleholder they stepped over that they were not the first people to venture through it. There were plenty of niches and crevices in the walls, but it was twenty minutes before their tunnel intersected with another passageway.

"We must be here," Meghan said, pointing to a

junction marked on the map where two tunnels met as Tia illuminated it with her torch.

"It feels like we've come a lot further than that," said Tia, a little dismayed by the short distance between Meghan's finger and the standing stone where they had entered the tunnel.

"Well, it's hard going, isn't it?" said Meghan, shining her torch on the jagged rock floor. "So it feels a lot further than it is. Look here, though…" Her finger traced further along the tunnel. "This is where this passage meets the one that leads to the crater where the stone fell last year. Let's head there."

Meghan was convinced they had established, beyond a shadow of a doubt, that the map recorded the network of tunnels under Stormhaven, and Tia could see no other explanation. So, confident that they would be able to find their way out without too much trouble, she followed her sister deeper into the underbelly of the island.

It wasn't long before both girls began to have their doubts.

Chapter Twenty-Four

The Ninth Stone

"We should have reached the other passageway by now," said Meghan after another twenty minutes of picking a path between the jagged rocks of the tunnel. "We can't have taken a wrong turn. There's only been that one junction, and we definitely went the right way there."

She stopped to check the map again, turning so that Tia could also see it. If it had taken them twenty minutes to reach that first turning, they should have passed the passageway they were looking for about ten minutes earlier.

A thought occurred to Tia. "Maybe we passed over it... or under..."

"What do you mean?"

"Well, these tunnels could be on different levels, couldn't they? They go all over the island, and the middle of the island is a lot higher than the outer bits. It feels like we might have been going downhill, now I think about it, so this tunnel probably goes under that one."

Meghan frowned, but nodded in agreement. "That makes it quite a confusing map, though, doesn't it?" she sighed. "How are we supposed to know which passages link up and which don't?"

"Are we lost?" Tia asked, feeling a rising sense of dread.

"Nah," said Meghan dismissively. "We can just follow this passage back to get out. There's only been one turn off, hasn't there? I'd like to know where we are, though," she added, peering more closely at the map.

Pasco had told Tia that the map this copy had been made from was centuries old, so it was very faded. Perhaps when it was originally drawn, it was more obvious which tunnels intersected and which passed over or under each other, but no matter how much Tia squinted at it in the torchlight, she saw no difference in the lines marking out the tunnels.

"I reckon," Meghan said, slowly tracing her finger over the map, "we must be about here. That means we'll be closer to an exit if we carry on going forward!"

Tia gave her a doubtful look, which Meghan couldn't see in the gloom of the tunnel.

"But that opening will be sealed up as well, won't it?" said Tia. "What if we can't open it from this side?"

"It'll be a lot easier to find from the inside. We just need to follow the tunnel to the end. I did bring a crowbar just in case," Meghan added cheerfully before setting off again.

Despite her misgivings, Tia told herself they would only need to follow the tunnel back the way they had come if all else failed. She bit her lip and followed after her sister.

They had not been walking for more than five minutes before Meghan stopped suddenly, causing Tia to bump into her.

"Turn your torch off a second," Meghan said, turning off her own.

Tia didn't want to be plunged into darkness, but she could see that her sister was peering at something further along the tunnel. When she followed Meghan's gaze, she thought she could see the faintest of lights gleaming in the distance. She flicked off her torch and, as her pupils slowly dilated in the utter blackness of the tunnel, she could see that there was indeed an unexpected glimmer of daylight further along the passageway.

"That entrance isn't blocked up, then," said Tia, thinking aloud.

Meghan switched her torch back on. "But how come no one knows about it?" she asked, consulting the map. "This entrance should be just on the edge of the village. Surely someone would know about it if it was open."

Tia flicked her own torch back on and edged past her

175

sister, taking the lead. She kept her light trained on the ground but glanced up regularly to see the dim glow at the end of the tunnel becoming gradually brighter. The sisters soon found themselves at the end of the passageway, peering out between strands of ivy dangling over an opening no bigger than their bathroom window.

Perhaps it was the blinding brightness of the day outside after they had spent about an hour underground, but for some reason Tia was reluctant to step out through the ivy. Meghan also paused, looking out through the tunnel entrance.

They appeared to be in someone's back garden. It was extremely overgrown with weeds, but the rusty table and chairs, and the untidy high hedges on either side suggested it was a private, enclosed space. There was an ancient, gnarled-looking willow tree in the middle of the garden obscuring most of what looked like an even more ancient and very dilapidated cottage. Its once-whitewashed walls had turned grey and its roof had lost almost half of its slate tiles.

However, the most surprising thing in the garden stood right in front of them: another standing stone. It was encircled by an area of tightly cut grass decorated with clumps of daffodils, which looked extremely neat and cultivated, in contrast to the unkemptness of the rest of the garden. Someone had woven a large hoop from stalks of willow and set it on top of the ancient rock, like a crown.

"I didn't know anyone had a standing stone in their garden," said Meghan, looking utterly bewildered. "The map doesn't show a stone at this entrance, even though it shows all the other eight stones on the island."

"Do you know whose garden this is?" asked Tia.

"No," said Meghan, shaking her head. "I might recognise it from the front of the house, but not from this side."

"It looks like we're right on the edge of the village," said Tia, noticing the cottage appeared not to have a neighbour on either side. "And it's pretty rundown. Are there any abandoned houses in the village?"

Tia would have felt a lot more comfortable stepping out of the tunnel if she could have been sure that no one was about to come out of the house and accuse them of trespassing.

"Hold on," said Meghan. "I wonder if this is—"

But Meghan stopped at the sound of an unexpected voice.

"Good morning, m'lady," said the voice from somewhere on the other side of the standing stone. It sounded as though the owner of the voice was an extremely old woman with very few teeth.

Meghan and Tia instinctively held their breath and took a step back in a bid to hide within the darkness of the tunnel.

"Spring is on its way, m'lady," croaked the voice.

Tia squinted through the ivy into the sunlight as the

owner of the voice stepped around the stone and into view. It belonged to an ancient-looking woman with long, tangled grey hair and a face with cracks and lines that matched those of the ancient stone. Her shoulders were hunched and she was leaning on a twisted wooden walking stick with one hand and carrying a wicker basket in the other.

As she rounded the standing stone, it became apparent that she was actually addressing the rock, casting cut white flowers from the basket at the foot of it.

"It's Mad Morag," hissed Meghan in Tia's ear.

Tia had never seen Mad Morag before, but she was one of Stormhaven's more infamous inhabitants, and Meghan had told Tia about her on the day of their first meeting. Tia had also heard her classmates mention the reclusive old woman, always with a mixture of ridicule and fear in their voices. Tia finally understood why. Morag undoubtedly had an air of madness about her; a madness that felt a little unnerving to be so close to.

"The air is warming and the flowers are beginning to emerge," Morag continued, having scattered her circle of cut snowdrops around the stone. "Yet each spring thawing seems to leave my bones slightly stiffer than they were before the winter set in." She cackled to herself. "I know not how many more springs I will be here to tend to you, m'lady. Perhaps this will be the final year." She sounded thoughtful for a moment, then cackled once more before turning back towards the rundown little cottage.

Once the old woman was out of sight, Meghan and Tia let out a sigh, each unaware that they had been holding their breath.

"Well, that was weird," said Meghan, stepping through the curtain of ivy. "I guess there are actually nine standing stones on the island. I wonder if anyone else knows there's one in Mad Morag's back garden!"

Tia followed her sister out into the daylight. Spring hadn't yet fully arrived, but the hazy sun on her face felt wonderfully warm. She looked at the rock, adorned with flowers and a willow crown, and squinted as her eyes adjusted to the brightness of the outside world.

"Right," said Meghan assertively. "Let's slip past the house and head home, shall we?"

She began edging towards the gate at the side of the cottage, trying to flatten herself against the untidy hedge and hide in its shade. Tia was about to follow her, but she stopped and moved closer to the standing stone. She stretched out an arm and laid a hand on its hard surface.

It was as cold and still as rocks should be.

Tia felt no tremor of life at all, and for some reason that puzzled her. She began to doubt herself. Perhaps she had not really felt anything earlier. Maybe her experience in Kirkburn had made her expect some sort of mystical connection to every old stone she encountered.

She was suddenly jolted out of her contemplation by an ear-splitting shriek that seemed to splinter the still air into shards of shattered ice.

"*What are you doing in my garden?!*"

Morag had emerged from a shed that was almost completely concealed by the overgrown hedge on the opposite side of the garden. Holding a flowerpot containing a long-dead plant, she was staring at Meghan across the wild lawn. Meghan was staring back at her in turn, and it was hard to say which looked more terrified.

But then Morag noticed Tia, whose hand was still resting on the standing stone, and her expression turned to one of outrage, her eyes widening in fury. "*How dare you lay a hand on the lady?!*" she howled.

"Run!" screamed Meghan, bolting for the gate.

Tia sprinted after her. She felt a swoosh of a walking stick swinging through the air as she passed the old woman and heard the smash of a flowerpot shattering against the wall of the house not far from her head as she dived through the open gate after her sister.

The girls didn't stop running until they had reached their own front door.

"Let's not mention any of this to Mum and Dad," panted Meghan with a hand on the door handle.

Tia nodded.

They took a few moments to get their breath back before entering the house as calmly as possible, given how hard their hearts were still thumping.

Chapter Twenty-Five

The Hollow Tower

The weather continued to improve as March progressed, and on the first still and sunny school day Mr Teague's Sky Class took the opportunity to get outside and play some of their favourite games. They began with gameball, a medieval game similar to football but with some use of the hands to catch the ball.

The original rules had been forgotten over the centuries, but Meghan and Bran had worked out some usable rules during a class project on games and pastimes in October. It soon transpired as they played, however, that the rules on how to tackle were still in need of clarification. After Gareth the Butcher executed a tackle on Aled that left him in a crumpled heap on the grass, Mr Teague decided it was time to try something else. So the class began playing Halo instead; a game Mr Teague insisted had its roots in an ancient Celtic sport that involved throwing metal torcs over people's heads.

Tia, Pasco and a few of their classmates were taking a break from the game, sitting at the side of the playing field watching two other teams play. Tia was thinking back to her first day at Stormhaven Castle School of Exploration and Discovery. They had played Halo that sunny September morning and Mr Teague had told her all about Celtic torcs.

"Torcs were what really showed how important someone was in ancient Britain, weren't they?" she said reflectively.

She seemed so engrossed in watching the game that Pasco was unsure whether she was just thinking aloud or wanted an answer from him. He decided to reply anyway. "I guess so. Why? What are you thinking about?"

"Well," she began, watching as Meghan grappled with Bran for possession of the Halo ring. "You know how we think the Round Table was a sort of medieval update on the Arthurian legends, where the meeting happened around a shield?"

Pasco could see where she was going with this. "You think the Coron Arthur might be an update of a torc worn by Arthur?"

"If the real Arthur wasn't actually a king, and crowns

weren't really the thing back then in Britain, a torc would most likely be what he wore to show how important he was, wouldn't it?"

Mr Teague was trying to straighten out the disagreement between Meghan and Bran over who should have possession of the Halo ring.

"So," Pasco continued hesitantly, "do you think it was a torc that Edward I put in the marble tomb at Glastonbury Abbey? Or do you think it was a proper crown, but it had no connection to the real Arthur?"

Tia puffed out her cheeks. "I have no idea," she sighed, watching Meghan stomp back into position while Bran gleefully twirled the Halo ring around his finger. "But we're going to Glastonbury this weekend; I talked Mum and Dad into a family day trip. I've no idea what to look for, but we haven't got any other leads."

"You could look for another Solomon's knot at St Michael's Church," Pasco suggested. "That worked before."

"We were looking for something hidden by Merlin that time, though; something hidden with magic. The Coron Arthur was hidden by Edward I or by one of the abbots of the abbey. This just feels different. It's like you said... it just doesn't feel so old; it doesn't feel like the *real* Arthur."

Mr Teague blew his whistle to signify that it was time for Tia and Pasco's team to play again.

"You should definitely still go to Glastonbury,

anyway. Even if you don't find anything, at least you'll know."

"There's something else that's bothering me," Tia said tentatively as she and Pasco rose to their feet to take their places for the next game. "I don't see how a torc would fit with the hallows poem Arwen Tresco gave me. A torc can't be 'that which covered his head to crown him' because it would have gone around his neck."

Pasco could think of no response to this, so he stayed silent and shuffled off to find a position on the playing field that he hoped would allow him to stay out of the way of the actual game.

The night before their trip to Glastonbury, Tia decided to bring Meghan up to speed on a few things she hadn't told her so far. She had already shown her sister the letter from Arwen Tresco and the Hallows of Arthur poem. As they lay in bed, having forgotten to turn off the light, Tia told her sister about the abbot of Glastonbury Abbey and how Henry VIII's men had executed him in their quest to uncover the secret of St Michael's Crypt.

"St Michael's is the church on top of Glastonbury Tor," she explained. "So tomorrow I want to have a good look around up there."

"Brilliant," Meghan replied with wide-eyed excitement. "There'll probably be a lot of people around, though," she said seriously. "If we do find something, we'll have to draw everyone's attention away from it. Do you want me to create a diversion?"

She looked so excited at the prospect of creating a diversion that Tia was on the verge of giving her sister the job, but she knew she needed to share one more piece of knowledge. She removed the Mantle of Arthur from beneath her bed and draped it over her shoulders.

"I was planning on using this," she said, pulling the hood over her head.

Meghan just about managed to stifle a scream as she stared at the spot where her sister had just disappeared.

"So it *is* magical!" Meghan whispered in awe.

"I only found it out by accident," Tia explained. "It's the hood that does it."

"Do you think we could both fit under it?"

Tia hesitated at first. She hadn't let anyone else wear it yet, although the only other person who knew she had it, Pasco, hadn't asked to try it on. It felt a little like the first time she had shown Mrs Trevelyan her thirteen treasures. In sharing something that had become so wrapped up in her own identity, she felt as though she was making herself frighteningly vulnerable once again. But somewhere along the way, Meghan had become someone she was comfortable being vulnerable with.

The pair managed to get the cloak around them quite easily, as it was so large, though they decided to hold it in place rather than fastening it around their necks. They were just about able to stretch the hood over their heads as well, and Meghan squealed in Tia's ear with great delight as they saw themselves disappear from the mirror on the wall beside their bedroom door. Moving around with both of them under the mantle was difficult, however, and after falling over for the second time they decided to put it away for a while and get back into bed before their parents came to investigate what all the banging was about.

Meghan drifted off to sleep, still chatting away about the secret entrances they were bound to find in the ruin of St Michael's Church at the top of Glastonbury Tor, no doubt marked with the same Solomon's knot symbol Tia had seen on the font at the church in Kirkburn, which she would be able to unlock in the same mysterious way she had opened the Chamber of the Thirteen Treasures. Tia felt a little uneasy about being attributed with supernatural abilities she was unable to understand or control. She clutched her pendant and listened to her sister's snores for what seemed like hours before she eventually fell asleep.

The next morning was crisp and clear, and it grew steadily warmer as they drove eastward towards Glastonbury. They had risen early in the hope of completing the long drive in time to climb the tor before lunch.

"It can get very busy up there, especially on a Saturday," Mr Trevelyan had explained, "so it would be good to do the tor in the morning. Then we can spend the afternoon in the abbey."

Tia did want to see the abbey, but after what her grandpa had said about the abbot's last words, it was the ruin of St Michael's Church at the top of the tor that seemed to hold the most promise. Yet Tia wasn't exactly expectant. She recalled how sick with anxiety she had felt on the journey up to Yorkshire during the hunt for the Thirteen Treasures. This time she wasn't even sure whether she was on the hunt for the right thing. As a result, the stakes did not feel quite so high, which was strangely comforting.

Tia was also sure that she had no better clues to follow, however, and it felt good to be on the quest for something. She recalled a November evening at the Jolly Dragon when Mr Teague had quoted something Ms Morgan had said to him about a quest being all about the journey, not the destination.

Nevertheless, the Trevelyans' little purple car reached *its* destination of Glastonbury after a couple of hours. Standing at the bottom of the tor, it seemed as though spring had sprung at last. The air was still, the sky was blue and the sun was steadily warming the March air.

"Now, it's not too far to the summit, but there's no need to rush it." Mrs Trevelyan looked meaningfully at

Meghan, who was hopping from one foot to the other in excitement.

Climbing to the top of a big hill was the sort of thing that would get Meghan bouncing with excitement on any occasion, so her parents thought nothing of it. But Tia could tell from her sister's constant winking whenever her parents weren't looking that she was incredibly excited at the prospect of finding treasure.

The air may have been still at the bottom of the tor, but it certainly didn't feel that way further up. The wind picked up and it seemed as though the clouds were gathering in around them as they made their way along the winding path that scaled the gentlest slope of the steep hill.

The route to the summit climbed a series of ancient terraces that Tia only spotted when her father pointed them out to her. They were covered in grass like the rest of the tor, and their edges had been rounded off by the centuries, but once they had been pointed out, Tia could see the level shelves of ground all around. She sensed the history of thousands of years of settlement on and around the tor, and millions more years of erosion before that, which seemed to make the air crackle with stories.

By the time they had reached the top, Tia felt as if she had been transported into a different world. The wind whipped around them from every direction and the sky was overcast. She pulled on a woollen hat to keep her thick curls blowing into her face as much as to protect her against the chill wind.

However, it was the view that made the place so otherworldly. There were no other peaks as high as the tor for as far as the eye could see. Meghan said she was sure she could see the curvature of the Earth across the vast, level land. It was as if they had risen above the world and were viewing it from a heavenly plane. The outward view was so commanding that it was a while before Tia turned her attention to the ruin of St Michael's Church.

A single, hollow tower now stood on the site, and the girls had explored it thoroughly within two minutes without finding a trace of anything remotely like a Solomon's knot or any other symbol. Meghan suggested one of them put the cloak on and climb the tower to see if there was anything up there, but Tia could see from standing inside the ruin and looking up that there were no crevasses large enough to hide anything other than the odd bird's nest.

Tia's heart sank, but she reminded herself that she hadn't expected to find much. She sat down on the grass and imagined the scene on the day the last abbot of Glastonbury Abbey was executed on this very hill. Was there really a secret crypt beneath their feet, the knowledge of which the abbot had taken to the grave with him? Or had he simply not told anyone because there was no secret?

Meghan continued to explore the ruin for a further

ten minutes before reading all the information boards she could find, then looking for ancient graffiti carved into the stones. But eventually she conceded defeat and flopped onto the grass beside her sister with a sigh. "So what do we do next?" she asked expectantly.

Tia simply shrugged and shook her head.

Chapter Twenty-Six

Among the Abbey Ruins

An hour and a half later, the Trevelyan family emerged from the little café in the town where they had just eaten lunch. They paused for a moment to get their bearings. Now that they had descended from the wind-swept tor, the day felt still and fresh once again.

Mr Trevelyan was just pointing out the large stone archway that marked the abbey entrance when Meghan called out to a young woman walking past with her face turned away from them. "Hey, I know you!"

The woman was wearing a university hoodie and a pair of jeans, which were muddied at the knees. Her long, straight black hair was tied back in a ponytail, and she was clutching a sandwich and a bag of crisps. She turned around with a slightly anxious look on her face that made Tia think she had been purposely looking away to avoid being recognised.

Not picking up on the young woman's anxiety, Meghan was beaming at her. "You're one of the university students who was at Stormhaven a few months ago!"

"Yes." The woman regained her composure and smiled convincingly as Mr and Mrs Trevelyan came over to greet her. "I was only there for a few weeks, but it was an inspiring place."

"Oh yes," said Mr Trevelyan, recognition dawning on his face. "You and a couple of your friends helped me catalogue those flint tools." Then he gave her an apologetic look. "I'm sorry, I'm not very good with names."

"Elaine," she said, continuing to smile.

"Elaine! Yes, of course."

Tia regarded the young woman carefully and soon recalled seeing her at Stormhaven. She had been among a group of university students Meghan had chatted to in the courtyard car park the afternoon they set off to investigate the church at Kirkburn for the Thirteen Treasures. Tia felt slightly sick as she recalled how freely her sister had told anyone and everyone about their trip.

"What brings you to Glastonbury?" Mrs Trevelyan enquired.

"Just getting some extra field experience during my Easter break," Elaine explained, fidgeting with her sandwich and crisps.

"Really?" Mr Trevelyan said, looking excited. "Is there a dig here in Glastonbury at the moment?"

Tia could see a plan forming in Mr Trevelyan's mind to drop in on the archaeological excavation.

"Who's leading it?" he probed.

"It's a small excavation at the abbey, led by a man named Mr Morris," Elaine replied, looking slightly nervous again.

Tia froze at the mention of 'Mr Morris', but reassured herself that it was a common surname.

"I don't recognise the name," her father said. "Is he linked to a university?"

"No, it's a privately funded dig," Elaine explained simply. "I should really get back. I just popped out to grab some lunch."

"We're heading to the abbey this afternoon, so we might see you there," Mrs Trevelyan said with a smile.

"Okay, bye." Elaine flashed them a weak smile and hurried off towards the stone archway.

As Tia watched her jog away, she couldn't shake the feeling that she recognised her from somewhere else.

The family followed at a slower pace, Mrs Trevelyan explaining to her husband that while he might be delighted to have a fellow archaeologist and their family drop in on a dig he was running, others might see it as an inconvenience. Meghan was firmly on her father's side, desperate for a chance to visit the excavation, but for some unknown reason Tia felt uneasy.

Glastonbury Abbey was hauntingly beautiful. Although there was little left of the original stone structure, the large columns and sections of wall that were still standing hinted at the cathedral-sized building that had once dominated the town.

The grass growing on top of the ruins whispered of the great tragedy and waste that demolishing the abbey had been. The immaculately kept grounds with their soft, even lawns gave the site a sense of peace and serenity that was a fitting memorial to the spiritual legacy of the place. She imagined how, for hundreds of years, the air around the abbey would have hung with the echoing chants of the monks. All seemed quiet and still in the fresh spring afternoon, as if the abbey had found a new, but no less spiritual, identity after the winter of its ruin.

The lady chapel was the most intact part of the abbey, and here they were able to descend into the crypt. Now open to the sky, the basement-level area was full of light, but Tia could imagine how dark and claustrophobic it must have been when the chapel was whole. She wondered whether there had ever been a crypt like this at St Michael's, and whether it had really held the Coron Arthur.

Narrow pieces of stone paving had been laid into the lawns around the abbey to mark parts that had once stood there but no longer remained at all, such as the cloistered square. The place that drew Tia more than any other was the centre of what had once been the main church. It was here that simple square slabs marked where the black marble tomb had once stood, built on the instruction of Edward I to house the bones of King Arthur and Queen Guinevere.

It didn't really matter to Tia whether the monks' discovery was genuine or not; it was a symbol of how a conquering Norman dynasty had sought to claim this Arthurian legend from the people of Britain, quashing the hope it gave in the process. Therefore, it was a perfectly appropriate place to mourn the Arthur she knew had once truly lived.

Tia had been standing beside the paving slabs as if she were standing before a tombstone in a proper graveyard for a couple of minutes before Meghan joined her.

"I've been thinking," Meghan said to her sister in a conspiratorial whisper. "If this is where Edward I put Arthur's bones, this is probably where he would have put the coron, too. But what if it was hidden right here and not moved by the monks during the Dissolution?"

"But what about the secret of St Michael's Crypt that the abbot died protecting?" Tia said.

"Maybe that was a red herring," Meghan replied with a shrug. "The best place to hide things is in plain sight. If it had been me, I'd have hidden the coron in a secret room right here under the ground."

"That's not exactly in plain sight," Tia pointed out.

"Ah, but the entrance would have been in plain sight." Meghan was getting quite excited, clearly convinced she was on to something. "The black marble tomb that stood here would have been the entrance to an underground crypt!" Meghan grinned in triumph, but before Tia could ask whether this notion was based on anything other than what her sister would have done herself, Meghan crouched down and began investigating the square slabs.

After some scraping of fingertips, she managed to lift one. "Hmm," she said, poking a thin stick into the earth beneath it. "It's just dirt directly underneath, but there's no telling what's further down."

"Probably more dirt," Tia muttered.

Her sister may have been sceptical, but Meghan was undeterred, and as they set off to rejoin their parents, she began wondering aloud what their chances of talking their father into an excavation at the site of the tomb might be.

After walking around all the grounds, the girls entered the small museum, where they found a model of what the abbey would have looked like, along with plenty of information about its history. Tia lapped up everything she could find about the Arthur connection but also became engrossed in the story of the last abbot, who seemed like an honest man who had been dealt with in a barbaric way by those serving Henry VIII. Whether or not he died protecting a worthwhile secret, his end had been tragic.

"I didn't see any excavation anywhere," Tia heard her father say to her mother. "Did you?"

"No," Meghan interjected. She stared out of the window for a moment, frowning, before spinning around and grabbing the sleeve of a portly man dressed as a medieval monk, who had just finished giving a tour to a group of French schoolchildren. "Excuse me," she said. "We were told there was an archaeological dig going on here at the moment. Do you know anything about it?"

The tour guide looked a little surprised at her directness, but soon smiled as people tended to when they saw past Meghan's brashness. "Why yes, I do," the monk replied jovially. "You probably missed it because it's happening under a big white tent over on the other side of the lady chapel." He pointed through the window towards the chapel.

"Ah," said Mr Trevelyan. "Beside the cloister walk, is it? I did wonder what that marquee was all about with its 'no public admittance' signs."

"That's right. They put a marquee up at the start of the week, supposedly to protect the excavation from weather damage, but I don't see why that was necessary, as the weather's been fine all week. It's all been very secretive really, but the dig's sponsor gave such a large donation that it was hard to say no, and they promised to share all findings with us at the end."

"Who's sponsoring the dig?" Meghan asked.

"Lady something or other," the tour guide said with a shrug.

Tia felt the hairs on her arms begin to stand on end. A secretive excavation, sponsored by Lady something, being conducted by someone called Mr Morris. It was far too much to be a coincidence.

"Do you know if they're looking for anything in particular?" Tia asked tentatively.

"Well," said the monk, who clearly loved sharing his knowledge with inquisitive tourists, "records and previous investigations suggest there was a tiny chapel just off the cloister walk, against the wall of the cemetery. This group's hoping to unearth what's left and find out anything they can about it." He paused and stroked his chin in a thoughtful manner. "We did think it a little odd that someone should approach us with such a keen interest in this rather obscure part of the abbey," he said, "but as I said, Her Ladyship made a very generous donation, and it wasn't going to cause any great inconvenience. So we said they were very welcome, and that we would be grateful to know anything they could find out about St Michael's Chapel."

"St Michael's Chapel?!" Tia and Meghan exclaimed in unison, gaping at the tour guide.

He was momentarily startled by the girls' reaction "That's right," he said after composing himself. "The records say it was a chapel dedicated to St Michael – not to be confused with St Michael's Church at the top of the tor, of course."

Chapter Twenty-Seven

The Forgotten Chapel

Tia and Meghan were under the Mantle of Arthur as they emerged from the crypt of the lady chapel, and therefore invisible to all. It was very awkward to walk side by side under the hood, both wearing backpacks, but the hardest part was getting up the steps that led out of the crypt. Fortunately, they didn't have far to walk across the lawn to get to the large white marquee.

They had left their parents in the museum saying they wanted to look around the grounds again. Being so enthralled by history and archaeology, Tia knew her mother and father would easily be able to spend another couple of hours cross-referencing and discussing every last piece of information in the visitor centre.

Tia's heart was still thumping in response to the discovery that the secret of St Michael's Crypt might refer to a location at the abbey rather than at the church on the tor. At least, Mr Morris and Lady Hendford certainly seemed to think so. Tia had made the same error as the abbot's executioners all those hundreds of years ago when they hauled him up the tor, demanding that he tell them everything he knew about the crypt.

Meghan was beyond her typical excited state of bouncing around manically. Instead, she wore an expression of steely determination, with a fixed smile that suggested a state of pure delightedness, and moved calmly. Tia was impressed and more than a little relieved by the way she was rising to the challenge. She had imagined her sister constantly hopping and squealing with excitement after discovering something so tantalising.

Still invisible under the cloak, they crouched down and listened when they reached the marquee. Apart from their own panting breath and beating hearts, all they could hear was the scraping of trowels against dry stone.

They slowly circled the tent, looking for a gap in the canvas that would give them a helpful view of the interior. This tent had clearly been selected for privacy, as it had none of the plastic windows that some marquees have, but two flaps hung slightly apart at one end. This, Tia guessed, was the way in and out.

The girls crouched down and peered through the crack. The sight inside was clearly that of an archaeological excavation, though the rectangular area being unearthed was a lot smaller than the tent. They could see two figures crouching in the trench, scraping away at the ground, and around the edges of the enclosure were tables laden with papers, trays of finds and a couple of laptops. On the grass by the entrance lay several shovels, a crowbar and various other tools.

One of the two people inside was clearly Elaine. The other was a well-built man with long, greasy hair tied back in a ponytail. He stood up when Elaine called to him, and Tia could see that he was several years older than the university student but younger than Mr Morris, who was nowhere to be seen.

"I've found it!" Elaine said.

"Found what?" the greasy-haired man replied, striding over to her.

"The entrance. See the edge of this slab? It sits higher than the other slabs on the floor. It must have been laid across the top of a staircase leading down into the crypt. Help me clear the soil away from the edge all the way around."

Tia and Meghan stood in an attempt to see into the trench, but all they could see was what appeared to be a stone floor at the far end. Elaine and the man were busily working away in a corner at the end nearest the entrance, where the sisters were crouching. They watched and listened, but could not see what they were working on.

After much scraping, Elaine fetched the crowbar and handed it to the man. "See if you can get that into the gap now."

She certainly didn't strike Tia as the junior member of this team. The man obediently did as he was instructed.

After working the bar into position, accompanied by the harsh scraping sounds of metal on stone, he leaned all his body weight against it. This time the scraping sound was stone on stone as they saw the edge of a large slab rise into view. Elaine stepped forward to assist, and the pair worked the stone all the way out of the trench.

Elaine leapt out of the trench to grab a torch, then stepped back in and shone it into the corner under the spot where the slab had been. The man was about to step into this lit area when the young woman placed a hand on his shoulder to hold him back.

"We need to tell Morris before we do anything else."

"But don't you think—" he began in reply.

"No, I don't." She switched off the light and stepped out of the trench again.

Tia and Meghan gasped as they realised Elaine was heading for the tent's entrance. The girls managed to co-ordinate themselves to step aside just as she strode past them into the sunlight. Then they held their breath as Elaine stopped and looked round in their direction, as if she had heard something. She was staring at a patch of air just above their heads, but her concentration was broken as the greasy-haired man emerged from the marquee and bumped straight into her.

She tutted. "Come on," she said, and the two of them set off towards the abbey entrance.

Meghan stepped through the open flap of the tent, and Tia had no choice but to go with her, given that they were joined at the neck under the cloak.

They were about to remove the hood from their heads when they heard Elaine's voice just outside. "Wait! You'd better do the entrance flap up first. We don't want anyone peering in and seeing what we've unearthed."

The girls froze as the man returned and began lacing up the entrance flaps to the tent. It was much warmer under the canvas, and they were uncomfortably close to each other under the Mantle of Arthur. Tia could feel the sweat trickling down her back, but they dared not move.

The man tied off the ropes that laced the entrance flaps together. It wasn't exactly burglar-proof, but it would take a while to untie and ensured that anyone passing the tent could not see what was inside. When the girls heard him walk off across the lawn they finally relaxed, breathing deeply as they took off the cloak.

"Keep the cloak handy," Meghan suggested. "We don't know how far they have to go to get Morris."

Tia placed the cloak back in her rucksack but left the zip open so she could pull it out in an instant if necessary. Swinging it onto her back, the two girls turned to look inside the trench.

Before them lay a rectangular area of stone slabs. The stonework looked very old, and Tia guessed it had once been the floor of St Michael's chapel. Around it was a border of rough and slightly raised stones, which appeared to be all that was left of the chapel's walls. The total area of the chapel floor was no larger than their little terraced house.

In the corner nearest them was a dark opening just large enough for a person to descend through. They could see a couple of stone steps that appeared to be the start of a small spiral staircase, but beyond that it was pitch black. Meghan grabbed two torches from a nearby table and handed one to Tia. They switched them on and directed the light down into the hole, just making out the end of the staircase at basement floor level. The descent looked very steep and uneven, and their torchlight illuminated nothing of the interior of the crypt.

"Are you ready?" Meghan asked, with the same exhilarated but determined look on her face.

Tia wasn't entirely sure she was, but she knew they needed to be quick. Sensing her younger sister's hesitation, Meghan offered to go first.

Tia held Meghan's hand as she stepped carefully down into the blackness. It soon became very difficult to keep hold of it, due to the steepness of the staircase. Tia had to crouch and stretch her arm downwards for

Meghan to be able to hold on from the bottom of the staircase.

It was a good thing she had managed to hold on to her sister, however, because when Meghan reached the crypt floor and shone her torch around, she recoiled at the sight of something and stumbled backwards. Squeezing her sister's hand to the point of eye-watering pain, she looked up at Tia. The determined exhilaration was gone. Instead, she wore a look of sheer terror on her face.

At first Meghan just mouthed some words, her voice taking a while to recover from the shock of what she had seen. When she finally managed to speak, it was nothing more than a hoarse whisper. "There's a body in there!"

Chapter Twenty-Eight

The Body in the Dark

"A stone carving of a dead person, you mean? You do get those in a crypt." Tia had seen pictures of stone effigies of deceased kings and noblemen lying on plinth-like tombs and thought it likely that St Michael's Crypt might contain something similar. Perhaps this was where the monks had moved the remains of Arthur and Guinevere to for safekeeping before the abbey was destroyed.

"No! I mean like a dead person sprawled out on the floor, as if he's been murdered!" Meghan looked white and her voice had become high-pitched and panicked.

Tia could see that her sister was frozen with fear and knew she needed to do something to help her. She prised her fingers out of Meghan's grip and shuffled a little way down the staircase, just managing to crouch into a position halfway down the steps that enabled her to shine her torch around the space below.

The floor was bare earth, and as she shone her torch on the ground, Tia saw the body that had so terrified her sister. Meghan squealed again as Tia's torchlight landed on the sprawled-out figure just two paces in front of them.

It was a skeleton that must have lain there, undisturbed, for hundreds of years. The ragged remains of clothes lay about the bones, and several rings adorned the fingers. Insects scuttled in and out of the bones, trying to avoid the glare of the light.

Tia could see why Meghan had reacted so dramatically. She was only able to remain calm because she had been anticipating a gruesome sight.

It felt eerily cool and the air tasted slightly stale as she breathed it in. The room appeared to match the size of the floor above. There was a sturdy-looking pillar in the centre to support the roof. Small stone archways linked the central pillar to each of the side walls, dividing the chamber into two halves. Each of the side walls was lined with the cross-shaped arrow slits often found in castles, and on the far wall there seemed to be a doorway that led out of the chamber, though the view beyond was largely obscured by the central pillar.

Tia rested a reassuring hand on her sister's shoulder

as she peered at the skeleton. A short, straight stick was poking up between its ribs.

"What's that?" Tia wondered aloud.

Meghan began breathing more calmly as she too peered at the object in the torchlight. "It's like a short spear – that must be what killed him. Maybe it was longer and whoever stabbed him snapped off the end," she suggested.

"It doesn't look snapped, though. I think it might be an arrow, though it's a bit short."

Meghan seemed to be recovering from her shock and regaining something of her determined look. "At least we don't need to worry about that any more!"

Both girls let out a sigh.

"Whatever's hidden down here must be through that archway at the far end," Tia said.

"The Coron Arthur." Meghan was grinning again now, albeit less enthusiastically than before.

Tia was reluctant to get her hopes up, but what else could it be? Perhaps she really was about to find another of the Hallows of Arthur. "My turn to go first," she said, stepping past her sister onto the earthen floor.

She shone her torch down at the ground in front of her where the skeleton lay, then up at the arrow slits on the walls. They were offset from one another so that anyone walking straight across the crypt towards the arched doorway would pass one on their left, then right, then left again. Then, after rounding the central pillar, they would pass three more arrow slits – on their right, then left, then right again – before reaching the next chamber. The person whose remains lay on the ground before her appeared not to have made it past the first cross-shaped window.

Tia knew there would no longer be archers waiting behind the arrow slits, but she still felt apprehensive as she picked her way around the skeleton and stepped into the line of fire from the first window. She held her breath and kept her torch focused on the first slit until she had tiptoed past it. Then she flicked her light across the crypt to the next opening on the opposite wall. She slowly stepped forward, but this time the torchlight glinted off something shiny in the recess behind the arrow slit.

Tia gasped. Thinking there must be someone there, aiming an arrow at her, she instinctively threw herself down to the ground. The earth shifted very slightly beneath her as she landed, and within a split second she heard a click and the twang of a string. Then something shot out of the arrow slit and cut through the air towards her.

Chapter Twenty-Nine

Crossbows in the Crypt

The arrow whistled through the air over her head and clattered into the stone wall on the opposite side of the room.

"Tia!" Meghan screamed.

Tia remained silent, holding her breath on the floor. She waited for another shot, but the hall was silent and still once more. "I'm okay," she said with a sigh of relief.

"There can't be any archers behind those holes," Meghan said, voicing Tia's own thoughts. "Maybe there's a tripwire."

"Yeah, the ground moved a bit when I landed just here." Tia scraped away at the floor in the dark, her torch lying where she had dropped it and illuminating the central pillar. Just below the top layer of dirt, her fingers found a flat wooden surface. "There's some sort of board under the earth that must have released the arrow from the slot."

"Quite clever, really." Meghan sounded genuinely impressed.

It was clever, but having just come so close to being shot, Tia wasn't really able to admire the ingenuity of it all at that moment. "What do I do now?" she wondered aloud.

"Stay down," Meghan suggested. "You'll be fine if you crawl. The arrows aren't going to be aimed at people's feet, are they?"

Tia felt this was good advice and decided to crawl along on her belly using her elbows to stay as low as she possibly could. She held her breath once again and angled the torch towards the next arrow slit as she crawled. She again felt a slight shift in the floor as she passed, followed by another click and twang. A second arrow whistled over her head, and Tia breathed another sigh of relief. She had made it to the stone pillar at the centre of the space.

She raised herself up onto her hands and knees, then sat on the floor, leaning back against the pillar. She felt as though she had just run up the tor rather than merely crawled a few metres along the ground. Tia looked back at her sister, silhouetted against the light flowing down the stairs behind her, and nodded.

Meghan got down on the ground, still eyeing the skeleton warily, and crawled across the earthen floor to join her in the middle of the chamber. No more shots came.

"Well done!" Meghan beamed down at Tia before walking over to one of the arrow slits and shining her torch inside. "There's a tiny gap behind the wall, just big enough for a crossbow. There's a string running down, which must be attached to the floorboards. It's amazing they still work after all these centuries."

Tia walked across to take a look, and then the girls turned away from the cross-shaped opening in the wall to shine their torches onto the archway at the end of the chamber. Standing to one side of the pillar as they were now, they could see through the opening. It appeared to lead into a second chamber, not much bigger than a cupboard, with a large recess carved into the rear stone wall at head height.

"It's in there!" Meghan sounded convinced, though they could see nothing inside the niche from where they stood.

"We need to get past three more crossbows first." Tia gestured towards the arrow slits beyond the central pillar with her torch.

She was about to step through one of the arches attached to the central pillar to the side walls, which appeared to be holding up the ceiling, when Meghan grabbed her.

"Wait!" she exclaimed, shining her torch upwards. "Look!"

Above their heads, in the underside of the archway, was a hole. It reminded Tia of the lessons Mr Teague had given on castle defences back at Stormhaven.

"Is that a murder hole?" Tia asked. "Do you think there might be another tripwire that'll drop something down on us?" She wasn't sure there was enough space below the stone floor of the ruined chapel for much to be waiting to fall on them, but she didn't want to take the risk.

"Might be." Meghan stepped back and aimed her torchlight up at the archway on the opposite side of the pillar. There was no hole there. "Let's go round that way just to be on the safe side."

Tia nodded and followed her around it. Then both girls shone their torches beyond the space guarded by the arrow slits to the doorway leading into the small second chamber. Something like a stone trough was sticking out above the doorway so that a visitor would have to walk underneath it to enter the tiny, cupboard-like chamber.

"A machicolation!" Tia said ominously, remembering the other style of castle defence used to drop things on attackers who attempted to breach the outer walls.

"Wouldn't Mr Teague be proud of us for applying what we just learned at school!" Meghan smirked.

Tia couldn't help but laugh, despite the circumstances.

"How are we going to get past it, though?" she said. "There's probably another tripwire ready to drop something on us as soon as we step through."

"I've got an idea," Meghan replied.

To Tia's complete surprise, her sister turned and ran over to the skeleton. She proceeded to remove the skull before returning with it clutched in her hands, grinning at her sister.

"You were terrified of that skeleton a few minutes ago!" Tia said incredulously.

"That was then," Meghan explained simply.

Once again, Tia was left to wonder at her sister's ability to live completely in the moment.

Meghan took careful aim, then threw the skull towards the doorway. It arced through the air, landing on the threshold of the tiny chamber beyond it with a nasty, bone-cracking sound.

There was a click and a scrape, and then a huge, square block of stone fell from the mouth of the machicolation. It crushed the skull with a horrible crunch, accompanied by a splintering sound as the wooden boards below buckled under its weight.

Meghan looked very satisfied with herself.

"Nice one!" Tia congratulated her. "I wonder if someone heard that, though."

"We should probably get a move on," Meghan said decisively. "Come on, let's go together this time."

The two sisters got down on the floor and wriggled

forward, side by side. As they passed each arrow slit they felt the familiar shift in the ground and heard the click, twang and whistle as the corresponding crossbow was released.

Only there was no whistle when it came to the sixth and final crossbow bolt. Instead, there was a loud thud as the arrow buried itself in the floor right beside Tia's hand.

The girls froze and stared at each other.

"We did say it was pretty amazing that they were still working after all this time," Meghan said with a shrug. "That one must have slipped a bit."

Tia tried to ignore the thought of what might have happened if any of the crossbows had slipped and shot at a slightly different angle, or if she had decided to crawl just a little further over.

Meghan seemed undaunted. She leapt to her feet, stepped over the stone and wandered into the tiny rear chamber. She shone her torch into the niche at the back and peered inside. "What on earth is that?" she said in a confused voice.

But Tia didn't hear her. She was too busy listening to the voices coming from above her head. She gazed back across the chamber of the crypt in horror as a foot appeared in the pool of light that was spilling down from the top of the spiral staircase.

"They're coming!" Tia hissed. "We're trapped!"

Chapter Thirty

Stumbling in the Dark

Without a word, Meghan switched off her torch and Tia followed her lead, plunging them into darkness. Meghan whisked the mantle out of Tia's open rucksack and Tia felt her drop something heavy inside in its place. Then she heard Meghan step past her into the larger, open space of the crypt. She pulled Tia into a corner by the wrist and arranged the cloak so it concealed them both. Holding their breath, they stayed as still and silent as possible.

"Where are the other torches?" they heard Elaine say from above them. "Well, here's one at least."

A moment later, a beam of torchlight illuminated the stone steps, and two feet carefully made their way down the ancient steps.

"Excellent!" said the owner of the feet. The torch shone a blinding light around the chamber, making it impossible to see the person holding it. But Tia recognised the voice as that of Mr Morris.

The beam swept across them twice, but the non-reaction of Mr Morris reassured her that they were hidden from sight beneath the magical cloak, as if they weren't there at all. Tia heard more footsteps on the stairs while the torch swept from the skeleton to the arrow slits in the walls.

"Booby-traps," chuckled Mr Morris. Using the beam of light, he located each crossbow bolt lying on the floor and matched it to its corresponding arrow slit. "They've *all* been tripped," he said thoughtfully.

"That's good, right?" It was the voice of the greasy-haired man this time, coming from behind Mr Morris. "That means we can just walk across."

"It means," said Mr Morris scornfully, "that someone may have beaten us to the prize at some point in the last five hundred years."

He directed the torch towards the archway leading through to the small rear chamber, which Tia knew he would not be able to see clearly from where he was standing. The torchlight began to bob forward into the crypt.

Tia nudged Meghan. The girls used the shuffling of the newcomers' footsteps as they crossed the chamber to mask the noise of their own. They moved carefully towards the staircase, keeping as far away from the adults as possible.

The torchlight suggested Mr Morris and the others had reached the arched doorway, and they hurriedly began investigating the tiny chamber before Tia and Meghan had made it to the central pillar.

We need to get out of here quickly, thought Tia.

Tia had been leading them around the opposite side of the pillar to steer clear of Mr Morris, completely forgetting about the murder hole. Meghan suddenly tugged her backwards, and Tia realised, just a little too late, what was happening.

"It's empty!" Tia heard Mr Morris spit indignantly, and at that same moment she heard a click at her feet. She heard a scrape of stone above, and felt something cold and solid brush the hood that hid her face as it thudded to the floor with a splintering of ancient wood just centimetres from her toes. Under the cover of the noise made by the rustling of stone and settling earth, the sisters hurried towards the stairs, stifling the coughs in their throats from the dust they had just inhaled.

The stone that had fallen from the murder hole was one of the slabs that had made up the floor above, and daylight now spilled down through the gap it had left.

"What the heck was *that*?" exclaimed Mr Morris.

Tia glanced back as they reached the bottom of the steps to see three shadowy figures examining the fallen stone slab.

"We can't both fit up the stairs under the cloak," Meghan whispered in Tia's ear before slipping out from under the hood and scrambling up the steps without the protection of the mantle's invisibility.

"What's that?"

Tia's heart leapt into her throat at the sound of Elaine's voice. She assumed they had seen her sister, but it soon became apparent that they were looking at something on the floor beside the fallen slab. Her relief was short-lived, however, when she saw that the object Elaine had found was the torch Tia had been holding. She realised she must have dropped it in alarm when she had narrowly avoided being crushed by the falling slab. She gasped and hurried up the stone steps as quickly and quietly as possible.

"Someone was here just a moment ago," she heard Mr Morris say from behind her. "Quick! Before they get too far!"

Tia tripped on the long cloak in her haste to get up the staircase, but managed to frantically scrabble out into the light of the large white tent. She glanced around, looking for Meghan, and was about to sweep her under the cloak before Mr Morris, Elaine and the other man emerged from the crypt when she stopped dead.

It had only been Mr Morris and Elaine down in the crypt.

The greasy-haired man had remained above, and was

standing between their escape route from the tent and a very visible Meghan. Both were as stunned as each other to have met in such a way and stood frozen to the spot, staring at each other.

Tia composed herself just in time to move away from the steps as Mr Morris and Elaine burst out into the tent. She made herself as small as possible against the side of the marquee and desperately tried to think of a way to get herself and Meghan out of this predicament.

"Ah!" said Mr Morris triumphantly. "Our little intruder!"

"*Meghan?*" Elaine looked bemused by the unexpected meeting.

Meghan glared at her defiantly. "Did you know you've been working for a criminal?" she said, then shifted her gaze to Mr Morris.

Elaine suddenly looked nervous.

"*You're* the one who's been caught in the act of stealing from a perfectly legal archaeological excavation," Mr Morris retorted, snatching Meghan's backpack from her shoulders. He dug around inside for a few seconds before looking up angrily. "Where is it?" he snapped.

Tia's thoughts leapt to the bulky object in her own, still invisible, backpack.

"There was nothing down there. The crypt was empty. Someone must have taken whatever was there years ago."

Tia was impressed by her sister's calmness as she

bravely protected the secret of St Michael's Crypt. She thought about the last abbot of Glastonbury Abbey for a brief moment, but that made her feel sick. She hoped her sister's fate would be less catastrophic than his.

"There may be two of them." Elaine spoke quietly, not looking at Meghan. "She has a younger sister."

"No one else came up while I was here," said the greasy-haired man.

"Tia's with my parents," Meghan quickly lied. "I snuck off on my own. Tia's a *good* girl," she added with a sneer so convincing that Tia felt a fleeting pang of hurt at her sister's words. "She wouldn't come."

Mr Morris stepped closer to Meghan, fixing her with an angry stare. He seemed unsure as to whether she was telling the truth or just happened to be a very good liar. "She may have left before we arrived," he said quietly without breaking eye contact. Then he shoved Meghan's backpack back into her arms.

"I'll go and hunt around. I know what she looks like." Elaine sidled past the others and out of the tent, still refusing to look directly at Meghan.

Meghan, in contrast, glared until Elaine was out of sight.

"What did you two find?" Mr Morris said quietly but forcefully.

"I already told you," Meghan replied with equal defiance. "*I* found nothing."

Tia needed to think of something, and quickly. Various elaborate plans that involved pushing Mr Morris down the stone steps or whacking the greasy-haired man over the head with a shovel passed through her mind, but in the end she decided the simplest plan was probably the best. She just had to wait for the right moment.

After a few seconds Mr Morris gave up on his interrogation and dragged Meghan roughly away from the entrance, telling the other man to stay there, blocking any means of escape. He forced her into a chair, then began searching behind boxes and under tables, checking that she hadn't hidden anything anywhere.

Tia silently edged round the wall of the tent until she was standing next to her sister. Then she bent low, so that her lips were as close to Meghan's ear as possible. "I'm here," she whispered.

Meghan gave a little start of surprise.

The greasy-haired man noticed and glanced at her, but had no reason to suspect that an invisible girl was talking to her.

"She looked really nervous then, Mr Morris," he said, "like you're getting close to something she doesn't want you to find."

Mr Morris grinned triumphantly at Meghan before returning to the box he had been rummaging through under the table.

"As soon as they're both looking away, I'm going

to put the cloak over you," Tia continued in a hushed voice. "Then we'll need to leg it to the other end of the tent. They'll think you've ducked out under the edge, so we'll give it a kick for extra effect. They'll run out and try and catch you, and as soon as they're far enough away from the tent we can slip out."

Meghan gave the slightest of nods.

After a minute or two, the greasy-haired man turned to see whether Mr Morris had discovered anything in the box. Tia instantly opened the Mantle of Arthur to engulf her sister in its folds. It was a little awkward when Meghan stood up, but her disappearance went unnoticed until Tia purposely kicked the side of the tent.

The greasy-haired man spun around on hearing the noise. "She's gone!"

Mr Morris banged his head on the underside of the table as he jerked up from the box he had been examining.

"How could you let her get past you?" Mr Morris shouted, rubbing the top of his head.

"I only took my eye off her for a second! She must have slipped under the side of the tent."

Mr Morris ran towards the tent entrance but was forced to stop in his tracks to avoid colliding with Elaine, who was just coming in.

"The younger sister is definitely not with the parents," she reported, looking as panicked as the others. "I think we've got an intruder on the loose."

"They're both on the loose now!" Mr Morris said impatiently, pushing Elaine aside. He didn't leave the marquee, however, because another figure stood in the entrance.

"I found someone else while I was searching for the little sister," Elaine said, looking extremely nervous.

Tia's heart rate had quickened numerous times that afternoon, as she had been shot at by a crossbow, nearly crushed by a stone slab and then her sister falling into the clutches of Mr Morris. But at this moment her heart almost stopped in horror. Surely there was no way this person could be re-entering her life at such a perilous moment.

"This is impossible!" Mr Morris said in a hushed voice, as if echoing Tia's thoughts. "You're dead!"

"Then this must be a truly terrifying encounter for you," came a slithering voice.

Into the tent stepped Mr Silverman with his sinister smile.

Chapter Thirty-One

A Ghost from the Past

"If you've lost the children," Mr Silverman said calmly, looking from the greasy-haired man to Elaine, "I suggest one of you watches the abbey exit while the other scours the grounds for them. So long as their parents are here, I doubt they'll have left the grounds."

The pair left without so much as a glance towards Mr Morris.

Meghan was pressed up close to Tia, who had tensed and then almost turned limp at the sight of this newcomer. Meghan had never seen Mr Silverman before, but seemed to have understood that his presence was not a good thing. She gripped her sister firmly, led the two of them to the far end of the tent in silence and waited.

Mr Silverman moved further into the tent and glanced casually at the staircase that led down to the crypt before sitting himself in the chair Meghan had occupied during her brief interrogation. He seemed completely at ease but looked older and more scarred than Tia remembered. His face was stubbly and his hair was a little unkempt; not exactly scruffy-looking, but certainly not as pristine as he had been the day he first appeared at Ms Davidson's house.

"Everyone thought you were dead," said Mr Morris, who looked decidedly tense and continued to gaze, wide-eyed, at Mr Silverman. "No one's heard anything from you since you went after that girl and the Thirteen Treasures. Where've you been?"

"You probably wouldn't believe me if I told you." Mr Silverman smiled and paused for a moment before continuing. "We found the Thirteen Treasures, but there was a cave-in inside the main chamber. I managed to get into a passageway with some of the artefacts, but Iago and Iolo didn't make it." He sighed and dropped his smile for a moment. It was as if someone had once told him about grief and he was making a half-hearted attempt at displaying the emotion without really feeling it. "If it weren't for them and their insatiable appetites I may not have survived, but they were kind enough to bring a few snacks along and leave them with our equipment just outside the chamber that caved in. Their choices did get a bit tiresome after a while, though. It took me a *long* time to get out of there."

"You're telling me you survived all this time on a few snacks your cronies brought with them?" Mr Morris still looked unsure as to whether he was talking to a living person or a ghost. "What about water?"

Mr Silverman gazed at him for a while, as if working out how much to say. Then he simply said, "I had the Drinking Horn of Bran the Stingy, the Knife of Llawfrodedd the Horseman and the Cauldron of Dyrnwch the Giant," as if that explained everything. "Although the cauldron wasn't all that useful at the time."

Tia knew the drinking horn would have given Mr Silverman all the drink he needed, assuming the treasures had kept their magical properties once they were out of the main chamber, as her cloak had. She recalled that the cauldron, knife and horn were the first items he and his henchmen had packed away, and it was their crossing the threshold of the treasure chamber that had triggered the cave-in.

Tia could imagine Mr Silverman in the underground corridor after the cave-in carving up the chocolate bars Iago and Iolo had brought in order to ration them out for himself, only to find them magically multiplying as he cut with the knife that could serve twenty-four men. She was sure the drinking horn probably could have provided him with much more nourishment than just water once he understood how it worked. Perhaps even a meaty broth.

Even if he had been kept alive by the magical objects, she wondered how on earth he had managed to get back above ground without the chariot, which had provided Tia and Pasco's escape. She had seen the font at the Kirkburn church back in its original position, guarding the entrance, so he could not have escaped that way.

Mr Morris frowned and scoffed at the mention of the magical objects, which seemed to amuse Mr Silverman.

"If you're cynical about that, I won't bother telling you the rest of my survival story." He laughed in a hissing sort of way. "It was a long time before I got back above ground, but I made sure I brought those objects with me, as they had already proved their worth. And when I did make it out, I spent time conducting a bit of research into them and the stories surrounding them before going to Lady Hendford just last night. She was most interested to hear of the artefacts, although I may hang on to one or two of them."

Mr Silverman looked down with an irritated look on his face and brushed something from his trousers. "I must admit," he continued, "I was a little surprised to hear that Her Ladyship had enlisted *you* as my replacement to track down her antiquities. I wouldn't have said that you and I were of quite the same ilk."

"Neither would I." Mr Morris's shocked look had finally been replaced by a look of contempt. "I'm an archaeologist and a historian. You are nothing but a criminal!"

"You're a criminal too, Morris," Mr Silverman sneered. "I just happen to be a *better* criminal." He seemed to be enjoying Mr Morris's obvious resentment. "That's probably why Her Ladyship suggested I come down here to assist you."

"I don't need your help, Silverman," spat Mr Morris with obvious loathing.

"Oh no?" Mr Silverman jeered. "My mistake, then. You're clearly in complete control of the situation. I have no doubt the two little girls who appear to have caused you so much trouble will soon be rounded up."

"And that'll be more than you managed, won't it?" It was Mr Morris's turn to sneer and Mr Silverman's turn to look as if he would have liked nothing more than to strangle the other man with his bare hands.

"There were more factors at play in Kirkburn than two troublesome children," he said coolly.

Mr Morris scoffed once more.

Mr Silverman scratched his chin thoughtfully. When he spoke again, it was clear that he had decided to change the topic of conversation. "Were there any 'security measures' down there?" he asked, gesturing towards the crypt entrance.

Tia knew what he was getting at. He was trying to determine whether Mr Morris had encountered any magical 'tests', as he had in the Chamber of the Thirteen

Treasures. It struck Tia for the first time that, unlike their trials in the Chamber of the Thirteen Treasures, they had come across no traces of magic whatsoever at the abbey. Also realising she hadn't yet seen the heavy object Meghan had dropped into her bag, Tia felt a sudden wave of curiosity. She wanted to examine this treasure to see whether it was truly one of the hallows.

"Crossbows triggered by tripwires," Mr Morris answered, "and a stone falling from a hole in the ceiling."

Mr Silverman thought for a moment or two before picking up a torch and walking towards the stone steps. "Mind if I take a look?" Despite asking the question, he clearly didn't feel he needed Mr Morris's permission, as he disappeared down the staircase without pausing for a reply.

"Go ahead," Mr Morris muttered to the back of Mr Silverman's head. "I'm off to look for those kids." He turned and left the tent.

The coast was finally clear for Tia and Meghan to slip out. Not wanting to risk being heard by Mr Silverman, they moved silently but quickly, knowing he might resurface at any moment.

When they emerged from the marquee into the open air, both girls allowed themselves a short breather before walking carefully towards the visitor centre and their parents. Closing time was fast approaching, so there were only a few people left milling around the ruins. Moving with them both under the cloak of invisibility was marginally easier than it had been earlier because they had abandoned Meghan's backpack in the tent, although the heavy item in Tia's was almost as bulky as the host of unnecessary items her sister had carried in hers.

"Look!" gasped Meghan, stopping them both still. "Over there, to the right."

Elaine was jogging down a path towards them, looking about her frantically. For a moment her expression seemed to change as she looked straight at them, but then she switched direction and moved away from them, speeding up a little.

Tia was about to let out a sigh of relief, but then she heard the quiet scrape of a footstep on the stony path behind them.

Awkwardly but silently, the girls turned.

Mr Silverman walked casually along the path towards them and stopped almost within touching distance, his snakelike eyes boring right through them.

Chapter Thirty-Two

Where Arthur Rests

He can't possibly see us... can he? wondered Tia.

After a few seconds, which felt like hours, Mr Silverman turned his head and looked in the direction of another piece of ruined abbey. Tia was almost grateful she had frozen with fear because Mr Silverman was so close that any noise at all would have given them away.

He was no longer looking at them, but he was still so close that the girls didn't dare to breathe. He sniffed and frowned as if he had just smelt something, turning his head back towards them.

Tia suddenly felt very sweaty. *He can smell us!* she thought. *And even if he can't, he'll bump right into us if he takes a step forward.* There was no way they could move out of his path without him hearing them.

Then, just when Tia thought she could hold her breath no longer, Mr Silverman turned and walked away to search behind another section of ruin.

Both girls breathed out as quietly as they could before sucking in a welcome breath of late-afternoon spring air.

Tia tugged on her sister's sleeve to suggest that they move in the opposite direction from the one Mr Silverman had taken. They paused in the middle of the open lawn, still just a stone's throw from the marquee, to make a whispered plan of what to do next.

"How are we going to leave without them seeing us? One of them's watching the exit and three are out searching the grounds!" hissed Meghan.

Tia couldn't think of an immediate way around this. "I don't know. What did you find in the crypt?" she asked as she mulled over her sister's question.

"I'm not quite sure. Let's get out of sight and take a look. I'm starting to find this invisibility thing a bit weird… and awkward. Do you think it has any side effects if you use it too much?"

Tia didn't answer, but she scanned the area for a suitable place to take the cloak off and examine the contents of her backpack without being spotted. She spotted a tea and coffee kiosk, which had closed for the day.

"Over there," she said.

"Over where?" Meghan asked. "I can't see you, remember."

"The coffee stall over there. It's closed, so we can duck out of sight behind the counter."

They hurried over, glancing around them for any sign of their hunters. Letting out further sighs of relief, the sisters crouched behind the counter, removed the Mantle of Arthur and slumped down onto the floor.

"What a team!" said Meghan in an excited whisper. "You were brilliant crawling under those crossbows and rescuing me in the tent!"

Tia grinned broadly at her. "Your quick thinking in the crypt is the only reason I wasn't crushed. And," she added, sliding the backpack down from her shoulders, "the only reason we didn't leave empty-handed."

"Don't get too excited," Meghan said, leaning forward as Tia undid the zip. "I couldn't get a good look at whatever it was in the gloom, but it certainly didn't feel like a crown."

The two girls peered into the bag and then frowned at one another. Meghan tentatively reached in and pulled out the treasure she had rescued from the forgotten crypt of St Michael.

She was right. It was definitely *not* a crown.

In Meghan's hands was a truly bizarre object: two bones that looked as though they came from human legs or arms, bound together with a twisted coil of gold that could have been worn on the arm as a piece of jewellery.

"Is that the Coron Arthur?" Meghan asked, looking bewildered.

Tia took the bundle and slowly turned it over in her hands, gazing at the golden object as she thought back to the conversation she'd had with Pasco while watching the game of Halo a few days ago.

"It's a torc," she said.

"I thought torcs went around your neck," Meghan replied. "This looks like it was worn around someone's arm."

"I reckon," said Tia, "that when it was first made it was worn around the neck in just one loop. But then it was twisted into smaller loops to wrap around these bones." She wasn't quite sure how this idea had occurred to her, but she was convinced that it made sense. "What if these bones are part of the remains that some monks in the twelfth century said belonged to Arthur and Guinevere?" she asked. "One from each skeleton? And what if this is the torc Edward I took after he conquered Wales. It was called the Coron Arthur, but it was still a neck torc when he got his hands on it. That's the sort of thing the real Arthur would have worn." Tia was getting excited as all the parts of the story seemed to be fitting together.

"Then," she continued, "either straightaway when Edward brought the coron to Glastonbury or sometime later, but before the destruction of the abbey, it was reshaped to hold these bones together; one of Arthur's and one of Guinevere's." To Tia, this somehow seemed like a rather beautiful medieval memorial to the king and queen of legend. "Then it was hidden to protect it. And that's the secret of St Michael's Crypt the abbots were protecting." Tia felt quite triumphant.

"But what about the poem?" Meghan said. "How does a torc worn around the neck fit with the hallows poem Arwen told you about?"

This was the same doubt Tia had voiced to Pasco, but she had thought of how this relic might fit with the poem. "Perhaps it's 'where Arthur rests'. It's all about Arthur's resting place, not his crown. Maybe the bones are what's important here because they signify 'where Arthur rests'."

Tia's triumphant feeling melted as she thought about one of these bones belonging to her historical Celtic Arthur. *That means he really did die and isn't lying in an enchanted rest in Avalon somewhere.* All of a sudden, her emotions turned to disappointment and grief.

But then another thought sparked; one that had been buzzing around her head for some time without really coming into focus. The whole thing just hadn't seemed as magical as the Thirteen Treasures, which made her wonder whether this really was one of the hallows at all. She still felt sure that this torc fitted with the history of the Coron Arthur and had almost certainly once adorned the neck of the great chieftain himself, but that didn't fit with the hallows poem, and the only magic they had experienced in St Michael's Crypt was that of the Mantle of Arthur, which they had brought with them.

Yes, there was plenty of mystery, and some quite ingenious traps had been protecting this treasure, but in Kirkburn she and Pasco encountered spells that had held back the passing of time and protected thirteen objects, all of which had supernatural powers. She had to admit that Sanddef the Guardian had never said that the Hallows of Arthur were magical – just that she had to find them. But it felt as though they should be a bit more magical than this.

And if this is the "where Arthur rests" hallow, maybe Arthur isn't truly dead.

She turned the bundle over in her hands once more and was startled when the two bones slid out of the twisted torc, straight into her open backpack. She was left holding what she believed to be the genuine Coron Arthur.

Was this really worn around the neck of Arthur himself?

Her thoughts were interrupted by the sound of a voice above their heads. "Aha!"

Chapter Thirty-Three

Escape

Wide-eyed with shock, they glanced up to see Elaine peering down at them. She instantly withdrew her head and the girls expected to hear her shout for Mr Morris. Instead, she rounded the counter and ducked down beside them before they had time to think about making a run for it.

"I'm not going to tell Morris or Silverman where you are, don't worry."

The sisters were taken aback by this.

Elaine was equally stunned when she spotted the golden object in Tia's hands. "So you *did* find something. Is that the Coron Arthur?"

She looked just as confused as Tia and Meghan had

a moment earlier, and she hadn't even seen the bones, which were safely tucked away in Tia's bag.

"Yes, we think so," said Tia. She quickly explained about her twisted torc theory without mentioning that the bones around which she thought the torc had been twisted were in her bag. "But why aren't you going to tell them where we are?"

"Because of Silverman," she said darkly. "I know Morris isn't exactly honest, but a lot of treasure hunters break the law to find what they're after. Silverman's something else, though. He doesn't care what happens to people at all. I thought I'd seen the last of him, but he's back. You have no idea what he'd be prepared to do to get what he wants."

"Were you spying on us at Stormhaven for him?" Tia asked.

"Yes," she answered, looking genuinely remorseful. "And it was me who broke into your house."

"That was you?!" Meghan said indignantly before Tia and Elaine both shushed her.

"He wanted me to find a pendant and twelve silver coins, although he wasn't totally sure you still had them. Silverman isn't someone you say no to," she said darkly, "so I'm going to let you leave with your parents." She glanced at the coron, which Tia was still holding. "You're going to have to give me that, though, or they'll come looking for you."

Meghan was about to protest, but Tia caught her eye

and silently shook her head. She handed over the spiral of gold and zipped up her bag.

"Let's go then," Elaine said rising to her feet and concealing the Coron Arthur under her jumper. "Morris was up near the pond looking for you a moment ago, but he'll be back down this way soon."

Elaine walked over to the visitor centre with them.

Meghan tried to have a whispered conversation with Tia as they hurried towards it. "What are you doing? Why are you giving up the Coron Arthur so easily?" Meghan clearly wasn't convinced this was a good idea.

"I'd *like* to keep it," Tia whispered back, "but we don't actually think it's one of the hallows, do we?"

"We don't know for sure, though," Meghan hissed urgently, "and we *do* think it's the torc of Arthur himself, remember?"

"I think it's an OK exchange for a chance to get away with the bones. I don't really want Morris or Silverman getting their hands on it, but I don't think we have much choice, do we?"

Meghan was so bemused she was rendered temporarily speechless, opening and closing her mouth a few times without saying a word. She eventually gave up her protest but still looked doubtful.

They found Mr and Mrs Trevelyan almost exactly where they had left them. Their parents looked as though they could have spent another hour in the small museum, but fortunately it was closing time anyway.

The greasy-haired man was standing beside the exit, but Elaine escorted them out, making polite conversation with the girls' parents as she did so. She patted the bulge the Coron Arthur made under her hoodie as they passed Mr Morris's henchman to indicate that she had found what they wanted. He looked a little confused but made no attempt to stop them.

Meghan clearly still had doubts about leaving without the treasure they had been shot at and almost crushed for, but she also said nothing.

They were soon sitting in the back of the Trevelyans' little purple car, heading over the Somerset Levels to Stormhaven.

Chapter Thirty-Four

The Burial

It was Sunday afternoon, and the first truly warm and sunny day of the year, though there was still a fresh March breeze blowing in from the sea. Tia, Meghan and Pasco had strolled down to the beach across the bay from the village. There were a few other people out enjoying the sun, but it was easy enough for the trio to talk about the events from the day before at Glastonbury Abbey without being overheard.

Tia had explained her reasoning to Meghan the night before, but they were going over it again with Pasco, who flinched as Meghan recounted the most dangerous parts of their crypt experience and gasped when he heard that Meghan had been captured.

Tia couldn't help but smile as her sister finished her dramatic retelling of the events.

"I guess it was a pretty amazing adventure," Tia agreed.

"Yeah," Meghan said in a dreamy voice. "It was brilliant!" She stared into thin air and grinned broadly to herself.

Tia could tell she was reliving it all in her mind.

"And we didn't leave empty-handed, did we? We got these." Tia patted her backpack, which contained the two bones that had been encircled by the Coron Arthur. She had mostly left them there because she didn't want to touch them unless she really had to, but she knew she couldn't leave them there much longer. She had no idea how she would explain it to her parents if they found two human bones in her bag.

"But you don't think they're important either," Meghan said, looking exasperated and slumping into the sand. "So we basically risked our lives for nothing."

"I didn't say they weren't important," Tia objected. "Whoever they once belonged to mattered just as much as we do. I just don't think they belonged to Arthur or Guinevere, that's all. They might have, but I think it's more likely the monks just made up the idea that it was Arthur's grave to make some money for the abbey."

When she had first seen the bones bound together by the twisted golden torc, Tia thought they had gone looking for one of the hallows only to find a completely different one. Rather than finding Arthur's crown – "that which covered his head to crown him" – perhaps they had found his grave – "where Arthur rests". In light of this, she had been willing to leave the torc behind and keep the bones, which seemed the more important part of the find. But after relaying this idea to Meghan the night before, her doubts had grown stronger until she felt quite sure her initial feeling was flawed.

"We never truly thought the grave was real, did we?" Tia said, retracing the thoughts that had brought her to her current conclusion. "We just thought it was the place where the real Coron Arthur might be hidden."

"And you were right about the coron actually being a torc," Pasco said. "I reckon that really must have been Arthur's."

"But a torc doesn't fit with the hallows poem, remember?" said Tia. "As we were saying the other day, you don't wear a torc on your head."

"But we also decided the real Arthur wouldn't have worn a crown, so what does the poem mean when it says 'that which covered his head to…'" Pasco stopped mid-sentence.

Tia waited patiently to see if he were about to reach the same conclusion she had.

"The Mantle of Arthur!" he exclaimed, leaping to his feet. "It's the hood covering your head that makes it work. That line must refer to the cloak. It's obvious when you think about it!"

"Yep," said Tia with an ironic laugh. That was exactly how she felt once she had worked it out.

"I still think the bones might be what you were meant to collect from 'where Arthur rests', though," said Meghan. "I mean, you can't collect an actual place, can you? So it must be something associated with his grave. His bones would fit."

"Maybe," admitted Tia. "I'm not just going to throw them away."

"But you can't really keep them in our room, can you?" Meghan said. "We'd have some serious explaining to do if Mum and Dad found them!"

"You think Arthur's just sleeping, don't you?" Pasco said to Tia, sitting back down again. "And that we need to gather all the other hallows to the place where he's sleeping."

"Yes," she answered simply.

Pasco shrugged. "After what we saw in the Chamber of the Thirteen Treasures, nothing would surprise me."

"Well, the torc and bones may not be important," Meghan said, lying back in the sand contentedly. "But like you said, it was a pretty amazing adventure."

After a happy pause she squinted over at Tia. "So what are we going to do with the bones?"

Tia felt she had needed to have that conversation with Pasco and Meghan – the only people who understood the quest that had been given to her – to settle everything in her mind. She hadn't exactly found any firm answers she could have recounted to anyone. She still didn't really know how to gather the Hallows of Arthur – or even what all of them were. And she still didn't know how or why she had been caught up in the whole thing.

But she felt different.

She felt she knew herself a little better, and she knew that Mr Teague would say that this self-knowledge was what really mattered.

After she had talked it all over with Pasco and Meghan, it seemed obvious what Tia should do with the bones. She should bury them. Whomever they belonged to, they deserved to be laid to rest with a proper burial.

So the trio returned to the wild slopes of the island, taking a brief detour to borrow a shovel from Grandpa Locryn's garden shed. Then, at the site of one of the standing stones that overlooked the sprawling ocean, they took it in turns to dig until they had made a small, deep hole.

There was silence as Tia knelt down, carefully removed the bones from her bag and placed them gently at the bottom of the pit.

They paused for a moment. At first it felt as though someone should say something to mark the occasion. Tia opened her mouth to speak but could find no words.

She wholeheartedly believed what she had said earlier; that the people these bones had belonged to mattered, whomever they were. But the fact remained that their identities were completely unknown.

She spent a couple of minutes thinking about the lives they might have lived, imagining them to be simple Romano-British farmers buried on the site of the earliest abbey at Glastonbury, only to be venerated as King Arthur and Queen Guinevere centuries later after the monks had excavated their graves. Tia had no idea if this was the actual history of the bones but creating a feasible story gave some sort of meaning to their burial.

Then Meghan picked up the shovel and filled the makeshift grave back in.

Tia looked up at the standing stone and recalled the day she had first met Meghan the previous August, when they had discovered the smugglers' hoard. For a moment she thought about searching this stone for a Solomon's knot carving similar to the one she had found that day, but in the end she simply turned to Pasco and Meghan and smiled.

"So," Meghan said, "where next on the quest for the Hallows of Arthur?"

Tia shrugged. "All we really have to go on is 'stone, oak, circle' but we haven't got very far with that. There are other clues we *think* are related, like the poem from Arwen Tresco, and the idea that the Round Table might actually be Arthur's shield. But the fact is, we don't know *anything* for sure."

Not for the first time Tia mourned the fact that the guardians of the Thirteen Treasures had been unable to relay all of Merlin's message. Mr Silverman had put a stop to that. Tia shivered at the thought of the man she had hoped never to see again.

"You have other clues as well, Tia," Pasco said in an encouraging voice as they turned to walk back down to the village. "Have your mum and dad found anything out about Brandubh? The guy Hemyke's landlady told you about?"

"I don't know," Tia answered in a surprised tone, realising she hadn't even thought about whether her father had made any progress with his investigations. "I guess not; I think he'd have told me if he had." She sighed. "That's got nothing to do with the hallows, though. We were just trying to find out where I came from."

Pasco looked a little taken aback.

"Surely it's all part of the same thing," he said. "Your story's wrapped up in the story of the hallows. You must see that! No one else could have found the Thirteen Treasures."

"He's right, Tia." Meghan looked as serious as Pasco.

"You're 'the key'. That's why you were named 'Tia Hemyke' in the first place, to fit the anagram."

Tia looked from one to the other. They both seemed astonished that she was attempting to separate her quest for information about her birth history from her quest to find the Hallows of Arthur.

"I don't know exactly how or why you're so connected to the Hallows of Arthur legend," Pasco said with a sigh, "but I know they're not separate things. You found the Thirteen Treasures while you were trying to find out about yourself, and I know you're going to find out more about yourself as you search for the hallows. And that matters more!"

"Exactly," Meghan added.

Pasco looked relieved that someone seemed to understand what he was getting at.

Tia was suddenly overcome with appreciation for her two companions and with exhaustion at the weight of her situation. Just a year ago she had thought of herself as an insignificant, overlooked girl, tossed about by the waves of unknowable fate on the margins of life. It had become clear that her identity was wrapped up in centuries of legend and magic, and she was now attempting a task that she had not asked for and did not understand or feel capable of completing.

Meghan placed a hand on Tia's shoulder and looked her in the eye. "We wouldn't be this committed if it were just a treasure-hunting adventure, you know.

Don't get me wrong, I love the adventure! But we're in it because of *you*, Tia. Because we believe in you."

And that, Tia realised, was the biggest difference between the present time and a year ago. She was no longer on her own.

Chapter Thirty-Five

The Mabinogion

The start of the Easter holidays a few weeks later was marked by the sort of day that promised a scorching summer to come, and the Trevelyan family decided to spend it on the sandy beach. As it was Good Friday, most of the adults in Stormhaven had the day off, and the whole village seemed to have had the same idea.

The water was full of people swimming, snorkelling, paddling kayaks or simply splashing about in the shallows.

"We should have brought the map with us," Meghan whispered to Tia as she eyed Merlin's Cave. The mouth of the cavern gaped invitingly from the side of the island across the water from them.

Tia knew her sister was still keen to explore the network of caves under Stormhaven. Meghan's sense of adventure, which had only increased after their exploits in Glastonbury, was making her extremely restless. Eventually spotting Bran Corentyn, she swiftly headed off with him and two of his brothers on their family's paddleboards.

Tia felt as though she would be quite happy without any adventure for a little while, though she knew that with several hallows still to find she was unlikely to have much peace and quiet for long.

She had seated herself on her parents' rug. They were both reading, although judging by the way Mr Trevelyan kept glancing up from his book to look longingly at Meghan and the Corentyn boys, part of him would have preferred to be doing some sort of water sport.

He and Tia spun around at the sound of an ice cream van that was winding its way along the track that led down to the beach. Mrs Trevelyan appeared too engrossed in her book to notice.

"Fancy an ice cream, Gwen?" Mr Trevelyan asked, rummaging around for his wallet and winking at Tia.

"No, thanks," his wife answered still not looking up from her book. "You two go ahead, though."

A queue had already formed by the time the van had reached the bottom of the track, and since most of the people lining up had been seated nearer than Tia and her father, they ended up at the back of the queue.

They were surprised to find themselves standing

behind Arwen Tresco. She was dressed very differently from the last time Tia had seen her, however. She looked very much as if she was on holiday in her shorts, T-shirt, flip-flops and large, round sunglasses.

"I was hoping to see you all this weekend!" Dr Tresco said after greeting them. "I travelled down last night to spend the weekend with Elowen. She's just over there, setting us up for the morning while I get a round of ice creams in."

Tia glanced in the direction Arwen had indicated to see Elowen Tresco struggling with a large beach umbrella. Commenting that it looked like a long wait, Mr Trevelyan suggested Tia and Arwen take a seat on a low stone wall at the side of the track while he waited in the queue.

"I was going to make sure we had a chance to chat while I was in Stormhaven," Dr Tresco said as she and Tia took a seat. "I've had some more thoughts about the questions you asked me in your letter."

"About the bards and the Hallows of Arthur, you mean?" Tia felt her heart quicken ever so slightly as she looked anxiously at Arwen, her mind suddenly focused on her quest once again.

"Not so much about the bards, but yes, I did have another idea about the hallows."

Tia waited expectantly for Arwen to continue while she rummaged in her bag for something.

"I still haven't found any other reference specifically

to the Hallows of Arthur anywhere," she eventually added, "so this may be nothing. But I started thinking about what the word 'hallows' actually means. Ah, here it is!"

Arwen pulled an old book from her bag. It was quite small – almost pocket-sized – and bound with a faded red cover. There were no pictures on the front of the book, but Tia could just make out the title in gold lettering: *The Mabinogion*.

"To 'hallow' something means to consecrate or make it holy," Dr Tresco continued. "And as a noun, it means the thing or person that has been made holy – like All *Hallows'* Day, or All Saints' Day, which is the day after Halloween."

Tia just about understood what Arwen was saying, though she wondered what the book had to do with anything.

"But what the word 'holy' really means," Arwen said pointedly, "is 'to set apart'. So I started thinking about any reference to the things of Arthur being set apart, and especially any occurrence of him setting something apart himself. That's when I thought of this." She stroked the book and leaned in towards Tia as she continued in an awed voice. "*The Mabinogion* is a very special book. It's about nine hundred years old – the oldest collection of British literature that still survives today – and the stories themselves are probably much older. One of the stories, "Culhwch and Olwen", is the oldest Arthurian story we have."

Arwen's eyes were wide with excitement, and it was hard for Tia not to become infected by her enthusiasm. She found herself leaning in closer as Dr Tresco began thumbing through the pages until she came to the place she had been looking for.

"It's wonderfully different from the better-known but much less Celtic tales of round tables and holy grails. It tells the story of a man called Culhwch, who tries to win the hand of the beautiful Olwen, the daughter of a fearsome giant. To do this, he seeks the help of the greatest chieftain in the land, Arthur, who also happens to be his cousin. Arthur agrees to help and says he will give Culhwch anything he asks for, apart from seven things or people he sets aside."

Arwen turned to the book and began to read. There were a lot of old Welsh names and the writing sounded very old-fashioned, which made it hard to understand. But Tia felt her skin tingle as Dr Tresco read in an almost mystical voice: "Quoth Arthur: 'Though thou bide not here, chieftain, thou shalt obtain the boon thy head and thy tongue shall name: as far as the wind dries, as far as the rain wets, as far as the sun runs, as far as the sea stretches, as far as earth extends, save only my boat, my mantle, Caledfwlch my sword, Rhongomyniad my spear, Wynebgwrthucher my shield, Carnwennan my dagger and Gwenhwyfar my wife.' So, there you have it: the boat, the mantle, the sword – which became better known in English as Excalibur – the spear, the shield, the dagger and his wife, whose name became Guinevere in English: the seven Hallows of Arthur." Arwen shut the book and shrugged. "Or that's my thought, anyway."

Tia was lost in her contemplations. She couldn't explain why, but this just made sense. It was everything the Coron Arthur hadn't been, and seemed to fit perfectly with the British Arthur who had once led the Celtic tribes into battle.

"Sorry," Dr Tresco said, mistaking Tia's thoughtfulness for confusion. "I may have got a bit carried away and not explained it very well."

"No, that all sounds perfect. But does that mean the list from the old Welsh bard's poem – the one you wrote about in your letter – wasn't really about the Hallows of Arthur?"

Arwen considered this before answering tentatively. "When you're considering legends and stories that have been handed down over hundreds of years, there are bound to have been alterations over time. Mistakes may have been made by scribes or bards as they copied or learned the story. Tales also evolve quite naturally with society, as each generation gives them their own emphasis – the same way Norman England reinvented many Arthurian tales, which became the most enduring King Arthur legends. But there are similarities between the two lists, like the weapons and the cloak being something that surrounds Arthur 'so that none can harm him'."

Tia was on the verge of explaining how the cloak was more likely to be "that which crowned him" but managed to bite her lip and nod in agreement instead. "So you think they might both be true?"

"I think a lot of people don't really understand what truth is nowadays," Arwen said with a sigh. "It's not the same thing as fact; it's so much more beautiful than that. Truth is like a person."

Tia wasn't sure what this meant, but Dr Tresco didn't seem to notice. She continued to talk with a faraway look on her face. "You can describe a person's height, weight, hair colour and various other factual things, or you can try to describe their character and the way they interact with the world around them. This is a lot harder to do, but it's so much more important. That's what truth is." She stopped and gazed down at Tia beside her, who actually *was* confused this time. "Sorry," Arwen said. "I got carried away again. Oh look, here's your dad."

Mr Trevelyan was walking over to them very slowly, trying not to drop any of the four ice cream cones he was carrying.

After handing over Arwen and Elowen's ice creams, and inviting Arwen over for dinner the next day, Mr Trevelyan and Tia said goodbye and headed back to their rug, licking their ice creams as they went.

For the rest of the morning, Tia swam a little and thought a lot. She was decidedly unsure about the hallows poem Dr Tresco had written to her about, but this new collection of items from *The Mabinogion* seemed to fizz with the mystical aura of the real Arthur.

The Penrose family arrived at the beach later in the day. Tia shared with Pasco all that Arwen had told her about the seven Hallows of Arthur as the pair walked along the beach, the waves lapping at their bare feet.

"She also said something about truth being a person," she added, "but I'm not sure I really got that."

Pasco frowned, quickly shrugging the thought off. "These seven hallows sound good," he said, "but we still aren't any closer to finding any of them. And how could we ever find his wife Guinevere, anyway?"

"Yeah, I'm not sure about that one," Tia admitted. "I can't shake the feeling that we're not going to get far until we work out what 'stone, oak, circle' is all about."

Chapter Thirty-Six

The Seven Hallows of Arthur

It was Tia who answered the door when Arwen Tresco arrived for dinner the next day. She used the minute they had alone to explain that her parents didn't know anything about her interest in the Hallows of Arthur.

"It's not really anything to do with what we wanted to know about Aneirin, Taliesin and the bards," she said, trying to play it down. "It's just something I got into."

"I'll give this to you now, in that case," Arwen said, pulling her copy of *The Mabinogion* from her bag. "I've got at least three copies at home. There's a bookmark marking the page I read to you yesterday." She handed it over with a grin.

Tia held it gently, as if it were a priceless treasure. "Thank you."

"There was something else I was going to tell you about Taliesin," Dr Tresco said casually as she hung her jacket on one of the hooks by the front door.

"What's that?" Tia asked, silently reminding herself that the manuscripts at the National Library of Wales had suggested a link between Taliesin and 'the key' to entering the Chamber of the Thirteen Treasures of Britain.

"It's nothing important, really," Arwen said, turning back to face her, "but the village I live in is called Tre Taliesin because it's supposedly home to Taliesin's tomb. It's just a local legend, though. The arrangement of rocks said to be the grave of the bard has been proven to date back thousands of years before Taliesin's lifetime. I just thought it was an interesting connection." Dr Tresco shrugged before heading into the kitchen to greet the rest of the Trevelyan family.

Tia lagged behind a little, frowning thoughtfully to herself. *It could just be an interesting connection, but might it possibly be more than that?*

She reminded herself that the grave of the guardians, Bryd and Sanddef, in Kirkburn had predated Merlin's gathering of the Thirteen Treasures by thousands of years. *Maybe it's just the name of the village that's important,* she mused. Tia's mind began to race with possibilities in terms of how she – the key – might be connected to this village named after Taliesin.

The next day was Easter Sunday. After a long discussion between Meghan and her parents about whether it was a good idea to have Easter eggs for breakfast or not, the Trevelyan family were just about ready to head off to the chapel up the hill. They were leaving the house by the back door when someone knocked at the front door.

"Oh, hi," said Pasco as Tia opened it. "I thought of something last night and wanted to come and talk to you as soon as possible."

"We're just off to church, Pasco," called Mrs Trevelyan from the kitchen. "Why don't you come with us and stay for lunch afterwards?"

"Er, okay."

Pasco's family didn't normally go to the chapel, and he looked a little nervous at the prospect. However, he soon relaxed into his pew, basking in the warm spring sunshine filtering through the stained-glass windows.

The Easter Sunday service was a good one to come to for the first time. It felt like a celebration of new life, and Grandpa Locryn talked animatedly about it being a season of hope and new beginnings.

As they walked back down the hill after the service,

Tia, Pasco and Meghan dawdled behind Mr and Mrs Trevelyan.

"It's about the Hallows of Arthur Dr Tresco told you about," Pasco said quietly as soon as there was an opportunity to continue.

Meghan wasn't one to let a conversation develop unless she understood all that was being said, so Tia had to bring her up to speed on the seven hallows Arthur had supposedly set apart in the story of Culhwch and Olwen. Seeing that her sister was growing increasingly excited, Tia promised to show her the original description in her copy of *The Mabinogion*, as she couldn't remember all the mystical names of Arthur's weapons.

"Anyway," Pasco said once Meghan had given him permission to continue, "I think the seven hallows might actually match the list of hallows from the bard's poem."

"How?" Meghan blurted out. "There weren't seven things in the poem."

"No, not in an obvious way. But 'that which armed him' could be three things: the sword, the spear and the dagger."

The girls looked at him thoughtfully.

Pasco took this as a sign to carry on. "We've already said that 'where Arthur held court, his men around him' might refer to his shield because they held meetings around the shield of the most important chieftain. And 'that which covered his head to crown him' must be the cloak, because it only makes you invisible if you pull the hood over your head."

"What about 'where Arthur rests' and 'that which enfolded him, that none might harm him'?" asked Tia doubtfully. "We've got to make those fit with his boat and his wife."

"You know the legend about Arthur going off to the Isle of Avalon rather than dying?" Pasco didn't wait for an answer before continuing. "I think 'where Arthur rests' is his boat, because that's how he got to Avalon."

"So 'that which enfolded him, that none might harm him' is his wife?" Tia said with raised eyebrows.

"Well, my parents' marriage wasn't all that great," Pasco muttered, looking self-conscious, "but that's kind of what someone you love and are married to is supposed to do, isn't it? Support you when things are tough? For better or worse, in sickness and in health, and all that."

"That's brilliant, Pasco!" beamed Meghan.

Pasco was still looking a bit awkward, and Meghan grinning at him didn't seem to help.

Tia gazed at her parents walking hand in hand ahead of them. She hadn't really considered it before, but their relationship did seem to give them the strength to face life's trials. She thought about how her mother had supported her father when they received the news about Nana Ollie's diagnosis, and could easily imagine Mr Trevelyan describing his wife as someone whose love enfolded him and kept him from harm. "So now we know what the seven Hallows of Arthur are," Tia said quietly to herself as she gazed up at the cloudless sky, soaking up the warm spring sunshine.

It suddenly felt like a season of hope and new beginnings, just as Grandpa Locryn had suggested. For the first time, Tia felt as if she knew what she was supposed to be looking for, although the idea of finding Arthur's wife was still rather baffling.

It was as if the hallows list from *The Mabinogion* and that from the old bard's poem were windows on different sides of a building that housed the truth of the seven Hallows of Arthur. It was a building with no doors, so she was unable to enter and physically grasp the truth, but she felt as though she could circle and gaze at it from different angles. Perhaps that was what Dr Tresco had been getting at when she said that truth was like a person, Tia concluded. She basically meant that truth was really hard to define.

Tia was still struggling with the fact that, even though they finally knew what to look for, they didn't really know *where* or *how* to find the hallows. They had no hope of finding either a mystical isle where Arthur might be slumbering in a boat or a woman who had lived fifteen hundred years ago.

She felt they still needed to work out what Sanddef's "stone, oak, circle" message meant. She also wanted to see if they could find any clues at Cadbury Castle hillfort – the possible site of the historical Camelot – and she knew they hadn't yet learned all there was to know about the standing stones at Stormhaven. *Do any more of them bear the Solomon's knot symbol? If so, should I touch them to see what might happen?*

Tia rubbed the symbol on the pendant she had worn for so long without knowing its secrets and smiled to herself. There were still so many unknowns, but for now, with a devoted sister and a faithful friend flanking her, and two loving parents ahead of her, Tia simply felt a quiet sense of hope.

The third book in the Tales of Truth
and Treasure series is coming soon.

Find out what Tia and friends get up to next in…

Secrets Set in Stone

All the books in the Tales of Truth and Treasure series
are available via emirapress.co.uk, amazon.co.uk,
or at a library or bookshop near you!

The Real-Life Treasures Mentioned in This Book

The Tower of London has been one of the most prominent locations in English history for centuries, and endless tales centred around this enigmatic palace are waiting to be discovered. The crown records are open to interpretation as to the fate of Llewelyn's Coronet and the Coron Arthur.

The National Library of Wales is a treasure trove of Welsh and British history and legend.

Glastonbury Tor and Glastonbury Abbey are more atmospheric than I was able to capture in this story and need to be experienced first-hand. The ruins and landscape exist as described here, although I believe a full excavation of St Michael's Crypt has not yet been undertaken.

Activities

There are oodles of potential cross-curricular links in the Tales of Truth and Treasure series that will provide readers with a more absorbing experience and enrich children's learning. Here are a few ideas for schoolteachers, home educators and curious readers that tie in with events in *The Forgotten Crown*. The activity doesn't need to be completed at the end of the corresponding chapter, but it won't make much sense to do it beforehand.

I believe that children learn best when their senses are engaged, and when their bodies and brains are stimulated. I hope these ideas will help my readers achieve that, and will inspire and excite them to dream, create, learn and grow.

Chapter One

Have you ever had a really vivid dream and tried to work out what made you dream that? Sometimes dreams are completely random, but at other times they reflect our feelings and put us in a place where we experience a very similar emotion to one we've felt while we were awake. Sometimes this idea is used in stories to portray a character's emotions in a slightly different way.

Think of a very strong feeling you had recently, positive or negative, then try to write or draw a short dream sequence that reflects it. A dream about being lost in a maze might reflect your worries about starting at a new school, or being on a train approaching an amazing fairground might reflect your excitement about an upcoming holiday or birthday. You could also make a dream jar using oil, water and paint to create colours that convey your emotions. The important part is that completely made-up experiences can conjure up very real emotions.

Chapter Two

Have a go at writing a holiday journal, either for yourself or for the days Tia spends in London. Mention the things you did, but to make it more enjoyable to read and write, describe how you felt about the things you did: what you liked; what you didn't like; what you wished you had done; what you feel inspired to do next. Include some photos and draw some maps.

Chapter Three

A few facts about the Tower of London and the Crown Jewels are mentioned in this chapter. Do a little research and see if you can find out more about the history of both and come up with some true or false questions you can put to someone else (this will be trickier if your false facts are just slightly altered versions of other true facts). You could also make some true and false cards for people to hold up when answering your questions and see how many they get right.

Chapter Four

Mr Morris seems younger in this chapter because he is walking differently – less hunched than before. Posture is one of the key drama techniques actors use to suggest the age or feelings of a character. Experiment with how you might move if you were three, twenty-three or ninety-three. Or how you might move depending on different feelings; for example, if you were surprised, ashamed, shy or ecstatic. Play charades where one person has to make another person guess the feeling simply by acting it out with posture and movement.

Chapter Five

There are lots of different methods when it comes to writing invisible messages. Try writing one using a white wax crayon on white paper, then using thin watercolour paints or food dye diluted in water to reveal it. Or simply write something, pressing hard on a piece of paper with a pencil, with a second piece of paper underneath to create an invisible message on the bottom piece that can be revealed by lightly shading over it.

You could also have a go at making some invisible ink using either milk or lemon juice with a few drops of water. Use a feather, toothpick, cotton swab or very fine paintbrush to apply your ink to write a message that will be revealed by exposure to heat (you can use a light bulb, candle or even an oven if you get the temperature just right, but only do this part with adult supervision).

An ultraviolet penlight would also work for most of these methods. Can you explain the science behind what is happening in these processes to reveal the hidden messages?

Chapter Six

Sometimes two feelings that seem totally opposite, such as excitement and anxiety, can be like two sides of the same coin, and actually be so closely related that we can feel both of them at different times about the same thing. Maybe you don't feel the same way about Christmas as Tia, but can you imagine looking forward to something but also worrying about it? Perhaps a residential trip, starting a new school or club, or thinking about the arrival of a new sibling?

Get a coin and label the two sides 'excited' and 'worried'. Think about situations where you feel excited. Turn the coin over. Is there sometimes a worry attached to those situations as well? What are those worries?

Chapter Seven

Nana Ollie gives the girls a list of things they should try to do to make the most of life: go on adventures, learn new things and so on. Make a list of your regular activities (school, clubs and so on) and some one-off things you have done lately. How many of the items on Nana Ollie's to-do list do they tick off? Can you think of some simple things you could do to tick more off?

Chapter Eight

You may not live near a library as massive as the National Library of Wales, but your local library is undoubtedly a gateway to countless adventures and discoveries. If you don't have a library card, get one. And if you do have one, use it! Even if your library doesn't have the book you want, the staff will do their best to get it for you, because libraries love sourcing books that they know people want to read. While you're at it, make sure your library has the complete Tales of Truth and Treasure series in stock!

Chapter Nine

Tia didn't get very far with interviewing Professor Hemyke's former colleagues, but what questions do you think she would have asked if she had been able to talk to them?

The question words 'who', 'what', 'where', 'how', 'when' and 'which' can help us form good questions. Assign each of the numbers on a dice a question word, then roll the dice and come up with a question starting with each word you roll (or write them on pieces of paper, fold them up and pick one at random), then think of a good question using that word.

Chapter Ten

Tia, Meghan and their mother spend a lot of time reading the names of Welsh people and places in this chapter.

Can you remember any of the Welsh pronunciation and phrases we looked at in *The Lost Child's Quest*? Here's a little recap:

c – pronounced 'k', as in 'kick'.

ch – pronounced as in the Scottish word 'loch' or the name of the composer Bach.

eu, ei – pronounced as the 'ay' in pray.

g – always pronounced as a hard 'g', as in 'get'.

i – pronounced 'ee', as in 'queen'.

ll – roughly pronounced 'hl'. Place your tongue firmly at the top of the mouth behind your teeth, then blow.

oe – pronounced as the 'oy' in 'toy'.

w – pronounced 'oo', as in 'spoon'.

y – usually pronounced 'u', as in 'fun', but pronounced 'i', as in 'is', in the last syllable of a word. So the Welsh for 'mountain', *mynydd*, is pronounced 'mun-ith', but the plural is *mynyddoedd*, pronounced 'munuth-oith', because the 'y' is no longer in the last syllable!

ae, ai, au – pronounced 'igh', as in 'high'.

aw – pronounced 'ow', as in 'cow'.

dd – pronounced 'th', as in 'breathe'.

f – pronounced 'v', as in 'of'.

ff – pronounced 'f', as in 'off'.

rh – pronounced 'hr' with the 'h' sound before the 'r'.

A few Welsh words and phrases:

Cymru (kumm-ree) – Wales

Bore da (bore-ray-dah) – Good morning

Nos da (Nohs-dah) – Good night
[Name] *dw i* (doo-ee) – I am [Name]
Helô/Hylô (hell-oh/hill-oh) – Hello
Hwyl (Hoy-ul) – Bye
Diolch (dee-olch) – Thanks
Croeso (croy-so) – Welcome

Chapter Eleven

Could you be a master storyteller like a bard? As with anything else in life, to accomplish this you have to practise. Pick a picture book you can read to a younger child, but practise first, reading it through several times to yourself so you can be really expressive. If you can tell a story without using a book that's even better, but again, practise first. Maybe you could film yourself telling the story and send it to a younger cousin or friend to enjoy.

Chapter Twelve

Meghan thinks the man with the guitar described by Mrs Gordan must have been a bard, and that he therefore must have known a secret about the Thirteen Treasures. Who do you think the man might be, and how does he fit in to the story? If possible, discuss your ideas with someone else and ask if they have any other thoughts. Be ready to explain your reasoning and see if you can arrive at an idea you both agree on.

Chapter Thirteen

Have a go at recreating the experiment mentioned in this chapter. You can find lots of ideas on the internet for making simple catapults and slingshots, using normal household items such as elastic bands, clothes pegs and pencils, or you could simply try throwing a ball at different angles.

However you decide to launch your projectile, try to work out which angle of release results in the greatest distance travelled: straight up in the air, flat or somewhere in between. Remember, if you're trying to find out what difference changing the angle of release makes, you need to keep everything else the same for each launch – for example, the same size and weight of projectile and the same power behind the release.

Chapter Fourteen

Find out about the early life of an adult you know well. Maybe you don't know anything about a grandparent's childhood or what your parents did before you came along. Invite them to afternoon tea (could you make a cup of tea and a cake to share?), then 'interview' them about their school years, their happiest childhood memories, their favourite food when they were young or what they did at the weekends. You might be surprised by how much life has changed! Don't badger them too much if there's anything they don't want to talk about, but there should definitely be a couple of stories they would love to tell you and that will be well worth listening to.

Chapter Fifteen

A few Arthurian legends are mentioned as Tia is trying to process the information in the letter, and she thinks there is a legend about Arthur being taken to the Isle of Avalon rather than dying. See if you can find out about this legend. A quick internet search might help, but there will also be plenty of books about the legends of King Arthur at your local library or bookshop. *Arthur, High King of Britain* by Michael Morpurgo is a great place to start.

Chapter Sixteen

Get hold of an Ordnance Survey map of your local area. The small dotted lines are footpaths, and there are probably a few near you that you don't know about. Go out (accompanied by an adult) and find a footpath you've never walked before. See where it takes you.

Chapter Seventeen

'Her Ladyship' is mentioned in this book and also very briefly in *The Lost Child's Quest*. Are you beginning to form an image in your mind as to what she is like? Try drawing or describing your initial impressions of her from what has been said so far.

Chapter Eighteen

A lot of historical events have been described in this story. Try mapping them out on a timeline. If you can do it to scale it will help to show how far apart some of these events took place. If you use a scale of 1 mm for every two years you will fit them on an A3 piece of paper, though it might be a bit crowded in places. If you use a scale of 1 cm per year it will be a lot easier to see, but you might need to go outside with chalk and a tape measure!

You could write the events on separate pieces of paper and play around with different scales to find one that works. Add some illustrations to make your timeline more eye-catching. Below are the events in our story, but you might like to add more modern events to put it all in context – for example, the Second World War or the year you were born.

1066 England is conquered and occupied by the Normans, who become the ruling class in the country.
1191 Monks in Glastonbury claim to have found King Arthur's grave.
1272 Edward I becomes King of England.
1278 The bones of Arthur and Guinevere are moved to a black marble tomb, under the direction of Edward I.
1283 Edward I completes his conquest of Wales, takes possession of Llywelyn's Coronet/the Coron Arthur and wipes out the Welsh bards.
1303 The Crown Jewels are moved from Westminster

Abbey to the Tower of London (and in our story, the Coron Arthur is interred with Arthur's remains in the black marble tomb at Glastonbury Abbey).

1307 Edward I dies.

1509 Henry VIII becomes king.

1536–41 The Dissolution of the Monasteries takes place, during which most abbeys and monasteries are stripped of all their property.

1539 The Abbot of Glastonbury is executed.

1547 King Henry VIII dies.

1792 The Gorsedd of Bards is formed in Wales to revive the tradition of the Welsh bards.

Chapter Nineteen

Bronze Age metalworking involved melting metals in a hot fire and then pouring the liquid into moulds to make jewellery or weapons. You might not have access to liquid metal, but you could try the same technique using a plaster of Paris mix and a hardened clay mould. Start by making a simple mould, perhaps by pressing a piece of jewellery into some clay, then work up to making some free-form moulds.

Chapter Twenty

With hundreds of ancient hill-fort sites scattered across the British Isles, there is probably one not too far from you that you could visit. However, as there will be nothing left but a hill and some earthworks, it's worth doing an internet search to find some pictures and descriptions of hill forts before you visit. When you do go, find a quiet spot and imagine going back in time. What might life have been like for the people who once lived there? Maybe you could sketch or act it out.

Chapter Twenty-one

Whatever you're feeling, it's OK to feel it. Wanting to avoid negative feelings is completely natural, but it's also completely natural to experience these emotions. Is there a feeling you don't want to face? Are you worried about something coming up in the future, or do you regret something from the past? When you're in a safe place, face up to these emotions and tell yourself, "Whatever I'm feeling, it's OK to feel it."

You could also play a game with a friend. Take it in turns to name an emotion (for example, jealousy, excitement, fear or anger). You each have a minute to write down as many situations that make you feel this emotion as you can.

Chapter Twenty-two

Meghan uses a compass in this chapter to check the direction of the tunnel. Make a simple compass using a needle, a magnet, a circle of paper or a cork, and a bowl of water. Rub one end of the needle on a magnet about thirty or forty times, ensuring you always rub in the same direction (not back and forth). Thread the needle through the cork or a small circle of paper, then float it in the water so that both ends of the needle are on, not under, the water. The needle will turn slightly and settle so that it points along the line of north to south.

Chapter Twenty-three

Tia and Meghan spend quite a lot of time working their way through brambles and ferns to find what is marked on their map. Brambles can really hurt, but they also produce delicious blackberries at the end of the summer, which can be picked and eaten fresh or used for baking, and new green brambles can be cut in spring to make lengths of rope to secure dens made from fallen branches. Leaves from ferns can be used for making beautiful prints simply by folding a piece of white fabric over them and hitting them with a rubber mallet. Have a go at one or two of these activities, depending on the time of year, but make sure there is plenty of the plant left to protect our wildlife.

Chapter Twenty-four

Like hill forts, ancient monuments and stone circles can be found all over the UK. Do some research to find your nearest site and see if you can visit it. Imagine what it might have been used for over the years, then use your construction skills to recreate it at home. You could use blocks, Lego, the contents of your recycling box or even cake!

Chapter Twenty-five

Find a local hilltop (again, an Ordnance Survey map might be useful for this) and undertake a little expedition with a parent or carer. Climb to the top, stopping along the way to enjoy the changing view. How high does the OS map say your hilltop is above sea level? Can you use the contour lines on the map to work out how far up you have trekked?

Chapter Twenty-Six

Reread the description of Tia's first impressions of Glastonbury Abbey ruins. Can you create a piece of peaceful music to complement the feeling of a spiritual sanctuary that medieval abbeys provided for so many people? Try listening to some medieval choral music first, then use any instruments that might be available or just your voice (singing or humming). It doesn't have to sound medieval; just peaceful. Keep it soft, slow and simple. Alternatively, you could try capturing some natural sounds that make you feel at peace, such as birdsong, waves or wind in the trees.

Chapter Twenty-Seven

This chapter features an archaeological dig. At the end of *The Lost Child's Quest* we had a go at trying to carefully excavate artefacts without damaging them. Here's an activity that focuses on another important aspect of archaeology: piecing together artefacts that are incomplete.

Gather a few old clay flowerpots, give them a quick clean, then paint a different design on each one. Place them all in a bag, then tap them lightly with a hammer a few times to break them up a little. Remove about a third of the pieces at random, then see if you can piece together what is left over to reconstruct the original artefacts as closely as possible. This will work even better if you do it with someone else and swap bags once you've broken up the pots you painted.

Chapter Twenty-Eight

Let's explore what makes archways strong. Try using blocks of sponge cake to build an archway that can stand up on its own. (Sorry, more cake. I love cake!) Can you build one that is able to support extra weight?

Chapter Twenty-nine

A crypt is an underground room beneath a church. Reread the description of the crypt in this chapter and draw a floorplan of it with the arrow slits, the central pillar and the second smaller chamber at the far end. Become a proper architect, using a sharp pencil, squared paper, a ruler and a set square.

Chapter Thirty

Blindfold a partner so you are invisible to them. Get them to count down from ten while you creep to a new position, then they should point to where they think you are. Would you be undetectable if you were invisible? Is it easier inside or outside? What types of flooring make it easier to detect someone's movements, and why?

Chapter Thirty-one

Make a survival diary for Mr Silverman, picking a few days throughout the months of his imprisonment. How do you think he felt as his time underground continued? There is still a lot of mystery surrounding how he actually escaped. What might have happened? Capture these thoughts in your diary.

Chapter Thirty-two

In this chapter, Tia explains how she thinks a sort of memorial was made from the bones of Arthur and Guinevere, and the Coron Arthur torc. People have many ways of remembering those who have died. Have a look around your local area to see if you can find any memorials. If you go to your local park you might see a war memorial or a bench that has been dedicated to someone, or a tree planted in memory of a loved one. Read any inscriptions you find and take some time to think about how these different memorials are appropriate in each situation.

Chapter Thirty-three

Before Henry VIII seized control of the Church in England and Wales, there were hundreds of abbeys and monasteries across the land, many of them playing vital roles in the day-to-day life of their communities. After he sold off their furnishings, land and most of their building materials, many fell into disrepair. Try to create a series of before and after pictures or photos of an abbey near you.

Chapter Thirty-four

In this chapter, Tia takes time to imagine the lives of the people whose bones have been venerated as Arthur and Guinevere. It doesn't matter whether what she is imagining relates to who they really were, because it helps make them real to her. Visit a graveyard and look around the gravestones, reading the inscriptions. Pick one that stands out to you (perhaps it is the oldest gravestone you can find, or one with a couple or family buried together) and create a backstory that fits with the facts you can gather from the inscription, so the person becomes more real to you. You can write it, draw it or just discuss it with someone else.

Chapter Thirty-five

This chapter never actually tells us what flavour of ice cream everybody chooses. What an oversight! Which flavour would you choose? Conduct a survey to find out the most popular ice-cream flavour, then decide on the best way of presenting your results. Will you ask people an open question – "What is your favourite ice-cream flavour?" – or will you ask people to choose from a list of options?

Chapter Thirty-six

There are still a lot of loose ends as this book closes. How are they going to find the Seven Hallows? Will Tia have another encounter with Mr Silverman? What secrets might be hidden in the network of caverns below Stormhaven? Will Tia ever find out how she came to be caught up in these legends, and what her true history is? What do you think is going to happen next?

Acknowledgements

Thank you to all those who have been so supportive of this book and of Tia's first adventure.

Thank you to all the teachers and home-educating parents who have shared this world with the children in their care and given them a taste of the Stormhaven Castle School of Exploration and Discovery experience. Thank you to the book bloggers, EduTwitter community and everyone who has shouted about the Tales of Truth and Treasure on whatever platform they have.

Thank you to everyone at Emira Press for believing in this tale, and for all the incredible work you've put into getting it out there. Particular thanks to Clair Lansley once again for the beautiful design work.

Thank you, Mum and Dad, for giving me a secure and loving childhood that enabled me to dream, imagine and believe.

Thank you, Rach, Lily, Tom and Benji, for all the adventures, without which I would not have been able to write the ones in these pages.

Thank you, Jesus, for helping me believe in the beauty – and bear the brokenness – of life.

About the author

James Haddell has always loved stories and adventure. He spent most of his childhood reading and daydreaming in Kent, then went to university in Durham to study maths and economics. Then four months spent volunteering for a Thai charity for children with disabilities in Bangkok after university changed everything.

James trained as a primary school teacher, working in various schools in London before getting married and moving back to Thailand for seven years, where he began writing the Tales of Truth and Treasure series. After adopting two children, he returned to the UK and worked in a number of primary school and nursery settings as a teacher and as a special educational needs and disability co-ordinator.

James currently lives in Somerset with his wife and three children, where he spends his time writing, teaching, and being a husband and dad... though he still finds time to do a little reading and daydreaming now and then.